A man with a dark baseball hat pulled low over his eyes roughly entered the hospital room, brushing past Dana with such force he knocked her off balance.

Before she knew exactly what was happening, the man rushed toward Mitch. Her eyes widened in horror when she caught a glimpse of silver near his hand.

Was that a knife?

Mitch reacted instinctively, grabbing the metal tray beside him and bringing it up to block the knife in the nick of time. The tip of the blade deflected harmlessly off the metal surface, making the man stumble.

Mitch used the tray as a weapon, bringing it down hard on the guy's head with a loud thunk. The man went down, sprawling inelegantly across the foot of the gurney. Mitch moved swiftly toward Dana, latching on to her arm.

"I need the closest way out of here," he said in a low, harsh voice.

"This way." She ducked out of the room, directing Mitch to the stairwell located just a few feet from his room.

"Who was that man?" she asked. "I don't understand what's going on."

"Frankly, I don't, either. But I have a bad feeling I'm being set up."

"Set up for what, exactly?" she asked.

Mitch was silent for a long moment, before he finally spoke. "Murder."

Laura Scott is a nurse by day and an author by night. She has always loved romance, and read faith-based books by Grace Livingston Hill in her teenage years. She's thrilled to have published over twenty books for Love Inspired Suspense. She has two adult children and lives in Milwaukee, Wisconsin, with her husband of over thirty years. Please visit Laura at laurascottbooks.com, as she loves to hear from her readers.

Books by Laura Scott

Love Inspired Suspense

Callahan Confidential

Shielding His Christmas Witness
The Only Witness
Christmas Amnesia
Shattered Lullaby
Primary Suspect
Protecting His Secret Son

Visit the Author Profile page at Harlequin.com for more titles.

PRIMARY SUSPECT

LAURA SCOTT

HHARLEQUIN® LOVE INSPIRED® SUSPENSE

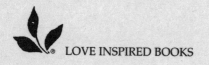 LOVE INSPIRED BOOKS

Recycling programs
for this product may
not exist in your area.

ISBN-13: 978-1-335-08120-9

Primary Suspect

Copyright © 2018 by Laura Iding

All rights reserved. Except for use in any review, the reproduction
or utilization of this work in whole or in part in any form by any
electronic, mechanical or other means, now known or hereafter
invented, including xerography, photocopying and recording, or in
any information storage or retrieval system, is forbidden without
the written permission of the editorial office, Love Inspired Books,
195 Broadway, New York, NY 10007 U.S.A.

This is a work of fiction. Names, characters, places and incidents are
either the product of the author's imagination or are used fictitiously, and
any resemblance to actual persons, living or dead, business establishments,
events or locales is entirely coincidental.

This edition published by arrangement with Love Inspired Books.

® and TM are trademarks of Love Inspired Books, used under license.
Trademarks indicated with ® are registered in the United States Patent
and Trademark Office, the Canadian Intellectual Property Office and in
other countries.

www.Harlequin.com

Printed in U.S.A.

Give ear to my words, O Lord, consider my meditation.
Hearken unto the voice of my cry, my King,
and my God: for unto thee will I pray.
–*Psalms* 5:1-2

This book is dedicated to all the brave men and women who fight fires every day, and especially those who lost their lives on September 11, 2001.

ONE

Fire Investigator Mitch Callahan cautiously approached the burned-out shell of a warehouse located on Milwaukee's south side.

Why had Fire Chief Rick Nelson requested a meeting here, late on a Wednesday night? Mitch had picked up the case after Jeff Walker's untimely death from a sudden massive heart attack and had already deemed the cause to be arson, despite the attempt to make it look like faulty wiring. He was sure he hadn't missed any sort of key evidence. His boss's voice had sounded strained on the message. Jeff's files didn't jibe with his investigational findings, so maybe this meeting was related to this disturbing trend.

Either way, he wasn't about to dismiss a direct order from his boss, no matter how unusual.

The pungent scent of smoke hung heavily in the air, something he was as used to as breathing. Stepping carefully, he crossed what had once been the threshold of a doorway. The interior was dark, so he pulled his flashlight from his back pocket and flicked it on, the narrow beam illuminating the interior.

"Hello? Anyone here?" he called, meticulously placing his feet around blackened two-by-fours strewn over the concrete floor. The place didn't look much different than it had earlier in the day, although seeing it at nighttime added an eerie dimension.

The interior of the building had sustained significant damage, but the metal walls of the warehouse were still standing. There were gaps in the metal roof from steel that had warped in the heat, wide enough that he could see stars flickering in the night sky.

This place had less damage compared to the two others he'd investigated over the past few months. Fire-damaged buildings were notoriously unstable, which made it doubly odd that his boss had requested to meet here tonight.

And where was Rick anyway? Mitch had been running late, but there was still no sign of his boss. Mitch stood for a moment, sweeping the area with his flashlight, debating heading back outside to wait.

A hint of blue caught his eye, making him frown. He aimed the flashlight toward the only bit of color amongst the blackened wreckage. He sucked in a harsh breath when he saw what looked like two denim-covered legs peeking out from beneath a pile of rubble way in the back corner of the building.

Was that a person buried under there?

His boss?

No, it couldn't be. The legs looked too narrow, as if they belonged to a skinny person rather than Rick Nelson's heavy-set frame. When he'd cleared the scene earlier that day, there hadn't been anyone inside. Besides, the blue denim wasn't blackened with smoke, so whoever this person was, he or she had come into the warehouse somewhere between five in the evening and now, nine thirty at night. Mitch moved quickly forward, just as he heard a noise behind him.

He started to turn around, but a second too late. Something hard crashed down, sending him sprawling forward. Pain exploded along the left side of his neck and shoulders, and he hit the concrete floor with a bone-jarring thud.

Then there was nothing but darkness.

Pain reverberating through his skull made him moan and shift, searching for a more comfortable position. Mitch abruptly realized he was lying on concrete rather than his bed. He blinked and found himself not far from a small flashlight lying on the floor.

His flashlight. It took a few seconds for him to remember that he had been at the scene of a warehouse fire for a meeting with his boss when he'd been hit from behind.

The side of his neck was wet and sticky with blood. With a groan, he forced himself to his knees, grabbed his fallen flashlight, then staggered to his feet. He had no idea if the person who'd assaulted him was still there, and his instincts were screaming at him to get out.

Now!

He took two steps before he remembered the blue jeans. No way could he leave without knowing if the person lying amidst the rubble was alive.

Sweeping his flashlight around the interior of the warehouse, he didn't see any sign of anyone hanging around. The blackened two-by-four that had been used to hit him was still on the ground, one edge stained with something dark and sticky, and he assumed it was his blood.

Moving as quickly as he could manage with his head pounding and his neck feeling like it was on fire, he made his way back toward the denim-clad legs. As he came closer, he could see the body was that of a woman with long blond hair. She was only partially covered with debris, so he leaned forward to feel for a pulse.

Nothing. He moved a two-by-four and saw the nasty hole in her chest, likely caused by a bullet. Her skin was cold, as if she'd been dead for at least thirty minutes, maybe more. He moved the hair away from her face and froze.

Janice Valencia?

Horror stricken by the fact that he'd once dated the dead woman, he recoiled from the body. He put his hand in his pocket to get his phone to call the authorities, when he heard the wail of sirens.

And suddenly he knew that whoever had assaulted him must have called the police. Was the intent for Mitch to be found here with Janice's body? For what purpose?

Nothing good. Mitch left the warehouse, stumbling toward his truck. He couldn't afford to trust the police, not if there was the slightest chance his boss had set him up. Maybe that sounded paranoid, but that's what happened when you found yourself alone with a dead body. Waiting for the cops and emergency responders to arrive on the scene wasn't an option.

Not until he understood what in the world was going on.

Dana Petrie looped her purse over her shoulder and slammed the small metal door of her locker shut so that she could reconnect the padlock. Exhaustion pulled at her, not uncommon after a long eight-hour shift. The stream of patients hadn't let up all evening, at least in team one, where she'd been assigned. Honestly, she had no idea what had transpired in the rest of the emergency department.

She left the locker room and crossed back through the department, halting midstride when she saw the familiar name on the ER census board next to room twelve.

Mitch Callahan.

Memories crashed through her mind, reminding her of everything she had lost just under three years ago. Her husband of barely a year, Kent, who'd died fighting a fire, and then her miscarriage on the day of Kent's funeral. Bile surged in the back of her throat, but she swallowed it down with an effort.

She would never be the same woman she'd been back then. Not that it mattered much; these days she focused her energy on saving lives rather than on her barren personal life.

She stared again at the name on the board. Mitch had been a firefighter, too, at the time. She'd heard the story, even read about it in the newspaper, about how he'd carried Kent's body out of the burning building and had instantly begun CPR. He'd fought hard to save Kent, but her husband had died in spite of Mitch's heroic efforts.

She'd never thanked him.

At the time, she'd been too traumatized by the miscarriage, especially on the heels of her husband's death. Then, months later, it had been easier to simply block the memories of the past, doing her best to move forward with her life, despite the twin gaping holes in her heart.

As the months turned into years, she had decided to leave well enough alone. But now Mitch Callahan was in the ER where she worked and her shift was over. Maybe she'd just take a quick moment to pop in to see him, check if he was awake enough that she could offer her gratitude before leaving for the night.

There was no reason to rush home; there was no one waiting for her to return from work. Not even a pet. Just a big, lonely, empty house.

One she'd grown to hate more and more with each passing day. Each time she wanted to sell, Kent's parents swooped in, demanding to know how she could leave the house she had once shared with their son.

She pushed the troubling thoughts aside.

Almost against her will, her feet took her toward room twelve, tucked in a small alcove at the end of the hall. Through a narrow opening in the privacy curtain hanging across the doorway, she could see a tall male wearing black jeans and a black short-sleeved T-shirt stretched out on a gurney. His feet, encased in black work boots, dangled off the end of the cart. The man had short blond hair and chiseled features. She easily recognized him as Mitch Callahan, which seemed a little odd since she'd met the man only twice before that fateful night. He appeared to be resting with his eyes closed, so she hesitated, loath to disturb him.

She took a step sideways, intending to leave him to rest, but her nursing shoes squeaked loudly against the linoleum floor. His blue eyes shot open and locked unerringly on hers.

No sense in leaving without talking to him now. She swallowed hard and forced herself to walk forward, entering his room. "Hi, I'm sure you don't remember me…"

"Dana Petrie," Mitch interrupted in a hoarse voice. "Of course I remember. How are you?" He moved to sit up, then groaned in pain. She could see that he had more than a half dozen stitches along the left side of his neck; the metal tray with discarded supplies was next to his gurney as if the doctor had left in a hurry.

What had happened to him? The jagged wound looked reddened and angry. She couldn't imagine what had caused the injury that had apparently brought him to the ER.

"I'm glad you came over to talk to me, Dana," Mitch said. "I forgot you were a nurse here."

"Yes, well." She took a deep breath and let it out in a whoosh. "I—uh—only stopped by to say thank you."

Mitch's eyes widened. "*Thank* me? I…always thought you blamed me for…" He didn't finish, as if unwilling to say her dead husband's name out loud.

"I don't," she said hastily, already regretting her decision to approach him. The last thing she wanted was to rehash the past. "You should rest. I just wanted to say thank you, that's all."

"Wait," he said, when she turned to leave. "Dana, please. I feel terrible about what happened that night."

"Don't." Her voice held a distinct edge. "I'd rather not talk about it. Just let me say thanks, okay? I hope you feel better soon."

"I will," Mitch said. "But will you do me a favor?"

She hovered near the doorway, eyeing him warily. "What?"

"Find out who my doctor is." Mitch eased himself up onto one elbow. "I really need to get out of here as soon as possible."

She wasn't sure why he was in such a hurry, but nodded. "Sure. You're in team three, which belongs to Dr. Crowley. I'll get him for you."

Before she could move, a man with a dark baseball hat pulled low over his eyes, his face covered by a black mask, roughly entered the room, brushing past her with such force he knocked her off balance. Her body smashed into the metal door frame, making her purse slide off her shoulder to bang against her hip.

"Oomph." Pain radiated down her arm.

Before she knew exactly what was happening, the man rushed toward Mitch. Her eyes widened in horror when she caught a glimpse of silver near his hand.

Was that a knife?

She opened her mouth to scream but no sound escaped from her tight throat. Mitch reacted instinctively, grabbing the metal tray beside him and bringing it up to block the knife in the nick of time. Discarded supplies flew everywhere. The tip of the blade deflected harmlessly off the metal surface, making the man stumble.

Mitch used the tray as a weapon, bringing it down hard on the guy's head with a loud thunk. The man went down, sprawling inelegantly across the foot of the gurney. Mitch instantly yanked his feet out from beneath the guy's frame, rolled off the cart and staggered upright. He moved swiftly toward Dana, latching onto her arm.

"I need the closest way out of here," he said in a low, harsh voice.

She was just as anxious to get away from the man moaning in pain on the gurney. "This way." She ducked out of the room, glancing around the ER. There were a couple of security guards gathered around a room where some patient was screaming in pain, loud enough to have muffled the noise from Mitch's room. She directed Mitch to the stairwell located just a few feet from his room.

The stairs only went up, because the ER was located on the street level.

"Who was that man?" she asked, leading the way up to the second floor.

"I don't know," Mitch said. "I didn't get a good look at his face, did you?"

"No, he was wearing a mask." She reached the top step just as they heard the doorway crash open from below and the sounds of heavy footsteps thudding against the stairs.

The guy was following them!

"Hurry," she urged, grasping Mitch's arm. "This way." She picked up the pace, running along a darkened hallway heading toward a stairwell on the opposite side of the building that she knew would lead them outside.

Where were the hospital security guards? She knew they had cameras posted in dozens of locations, mostly in the main thoroughfares, not in patient rooms. Still, someone must have noticed them fleeing from a guy with a knife.

But the only sounds echoing around them were their own footsteps and their own heavy breathing.

If she was on speaking terms with God, she might have prayed, but the words wouldn't form in her mind. Instead, she focused on moving as fast as possible away from the man threatening them.

The minute they cleared the doorway of the stairwell across the hall, Mitch caught the door, making sure it closed soundlessly behind them. She understood he was trying to hide their location from the knife-wielding guy following them, so she did her best to step quietly as she headed back down to the main level of the hospital.

Moments later, they burst through the lower level of the stairwell, into the balmy summer night. It felt good to be outside the constricting walls of the building.

"Do you have a car here?" Mitch asked.

"Of course. But shouldn't we talk to the police?"

"No. We need to get out of here."

She hesitated, unsure of why he was in such a hurry to leave without notifying the authorities. The adrenaline rushing through her veins ebbed away, leaving her feeling weak and shaky.

"Okay, fine. This way," she said, gesturing for him to follow her across the surface parking lot to the concrete structure looming before them.

Mitch positioned himself behind her as she wove through the parked cars to the spot where she'd left her small two-door sedan.

She dug into her purse for her keys, using the fob to unlock the vehicle. She slid behind the wheel, leaving Mitch to fold himself into the passenger seat. The area along the side of his neck was awash with fresh blood, and she realized he must have broken open his stitches.

"You're bleeding. We need to get you back inside," she said, turning toward him. "You'll need several of those sutures repaired."

"No time. Let's go. Hurry!"

With a sigh she started the engine and backed out of the parking space. As soon as she put the car in Drive and rolled forward, she saw him.

The guy wearing the face mask was sprinting across the open parking area, heading straight toward them, his hand still gripping the knife.

"Go, go, go!" Mitch shouted.

She hit the accelerator and sent the car flying through the structure. She took a corner, heading away from the man, which also brought them closer to the exit. Thankfully, she was on the first floor and the gate was up, so she didn't have to slow down too much.

After exiting the structure, she cranked the wheel hard to the right, taking them far away from the bright lights of the hospital into the inky darkness. Risking a glance at her rearview mirror, she tried to see where the guy was.

There was no sign of him. Her shoulders slumped in relief, until it hit her.

Obviously, he must have a car there, too. Was he right now jumping inside to follow them?

"Take another right," Mitch said, drawing her attention from the knife guy. "The freeway on-ramp isn't far."

"The freeway?" She glanced at him in confusion. "Where are we going?"

"Anywhere. Preferably as far away from this hospital as possible," he muttered in a grim tone. "We need to make sure he hasn't followed us."

She couldn't deny she wanted the exact same thing. She drove through the night, the bitter taste of fear coating her tongue.

The events that had taken place in the past few minutes seemed unreal. The more she thought about it, the less it made sense.

"But why?" she pressed, tightening her grip on the steering wheel. "Why would he follow us? I don't understand what's going on."

"Frankly, I don't, either." Mitch tentatively felt along the side of his neck, where the oozing blood was beginning to congeal into a tacky mess. "But I have a bad feeling I'm being set up."

She took the on-ramp and pressed the accelerator down to get up to freeway speed. As her compact car ate up the miles, her thoughts whirled.

Had Mitch suffered some kind of head injury? Or was he just being paranoid? There was no denying the knife-wielding guy had intended to cause him harm, but to show up at the hospital? Who did that? This whole situation was downright crazy.

"Set up for what, exactly?" she asked.

Mitch was silent for a long moment before he finally spoke. "Murder."

TWO

Bracing himself with one hand wedged against the glove compartment, Mitch scanned the area, trying to think of a way out of this disastrous turn of events.

He hated the fact that he'd dragged sweet Dana Petrie into it, too, but there hadn't been another option. No way was he leaving her behind. Not considering that his assailant knew what she looked like. Although there had been something about the way he moved that seemed familiar. If only he'd gotten a look at his face.

"Murder?" Dana's voice rose a notch. "What are you talking about?"

There were several sets of headlights behind them, making him nervous. What if one of them belonged to his attacker? "Take the next exit," he directed. "We need to change directions."

"No." Dana's mouth thinned into a stubborn line. She'd cut her blue-black hair since the last time he'd seen her, wearing it in a chin-length silky bob that accented her dainty features. She was as beautiful as he remembered. "I'm not driving around willy-nilly until you tell me exactly what's going on. Why do you think you're being set up for murder?"

He ignored the ache in his head and forced himself

to concentrate. "Please," he said in a low voice. "Please take the next exit. I promise I'll explain everything, but I need to be certain that man isn't following us."

"Fine," she muttered harshly, taking her foot off the accelerator and heading toward the exit. "Happy? Now start talking."

"I was attacked earlier this evening at the site of a warehouse fire," Mitch said. "Just before I was hit from behind, I saw a pair of jean-clad legs sticking out from a pile of rubble."

She stopped at a stoplight, then turned to face him. "What makes you think the body was a result of murder?"

"The light's turned green," he said.

She scowled and hit the gas. "You're not making any sense."

He rubbed his temple and acknowledged she was right. He needed to start at the very beginning. "My boss, Fire Chief Rick Nelson, left me a message telling me to meet him at the warehouse at nine," he explained. "I didn't get the message right away, so I was almost thirty minutes late. When I arrived at the warehouse, which also happened to be the site of a recent fire that I deemed to be caused by arson, I thought the place was empty. But then I went inside and saw a pair of jean-clad legs in the beam of my flashlight. Before I could go over to investigate, someone hit me from behind. I turned, so the strike connected along the side of my neck and shoulder, but there was enough force that I fell to the ground. My head bounced on the concrete." He gingerly felt along the back of his head, fingering a lump the size of a golf ball.

"Should I keep going straight? Or head west?" Dana asked when she came to the next intersection.

"West." He didn't have a destination in mind, other than to avoid going to his place or hers. There was the slim possibility that the guy chasing them might have gotten her license plate number.

"I still don't understand." Dana turned the steering wheel to head west. "The police are notified for each ambulance call. They would have met up with you here in the ER and would have placed you under arrest if you were suspected of murder."

"I'm aware of how it works," he said in a dry tone. "A few of my brothers are cops. Thankfully, I only blacked out for a few minutes. When I came to, I went over to check on the person lying half buried in the debris. The body was that of a young woman with long blond hair, and she was dead from a gunshot wound to her chest." He wasn't quite ready to admit that he not only knew the dead woman but had dated her a year earlier. "I heard the sirens and knew that whoever had hit me must have called the police. I managed to get away before they arrived."

"You drove yourself to the hospital," she concluded.

"Yes. My goal was to get stitched up and quickly discharged. I didn't anticipate that I'd be found and attacked again." He was ticked off at how ruthlessly the guy had come after him, not even caring about injuring an innocent woman in the process. Then again, maybe he was the same guy who'd murdered Janice Valencia in the first place? If that was the case, the guy was capable of anything. "I'm sorry for dragging you into this mess."

"It's hardly your fault," she said, but her tone lacked conviction. "Do you want me to take you home?"

He closed his eyes and shook his head. "I can't go home. This guy obviously knows who I am. Which means he'll easily be able to figure out where I live. I have no idea why someone has decided to frame me, but it must involve the dead girl somehow."

"Okay, so where to, then?" Thinly veiled frustration convinced him that Dana was clearly anxious to get rid of him, not that he could blame her.

"Maybe a motel," he said, thinking out loud.

"A motel?" She raised an eyebrow. "Why not get in touch with your family?"

"I'm not putting them in danger." He considered giving Miles a call, but it was already approaching midnight. Better to wait until morning. Miles was a Milwaukee homicide detective, but he also happened to have his hands full with a new baby son.

His other brother, Matt, was a K-9 officer but he was currently on his honeymoon with his new bride, Lacy. His mother and grandmother were taking care of Rory, Lacy's newly adopted son, and Duchess, Matt's canine partner.

Dana let out a heavy sigh. "Okay, fine. There's no need to stay in a motel. You can bunk at my place. But only until the morning, understand?"

As much as he was touched by her offer, there was no way she was going home, either. "Listen, Dana, I need you to understand that you could be in danger now, too. Unfortunately, I can't let you go home. Not yet. It's not safe."

The car swerved as she turned to gape at him. "What are you talking about? I'm not the target here, you are. This is *your* problem, Mitch Callahan, not mine!"

He winced, wishing there was something he could say to smooth things over. Wasn't it bad enough that he'd failed to save her rookie firefighter husband's life three years ago? To think she'd actually come over to thank him, only to be placed in harm's way!

"I'm sorry, Dana. But I think we have to assume the guy may have gotten your license plate number."

"So what if he did? Are you saying he has the connections to find my home address? To track me down?"

She had a point, but he couldn't get over the fact that his boss had been the one to set up the meeting at the warehouse. Especially after handing him all of Jeff Walker's cases where he'd found several irregularities. What did it mean? Why would Rick try to set him up? Or had the phone call been someone pretending to be his boss? No, that didn't make sense, either; the call had come from Rick's office number. Not many people had access to the office of the fire chief.

The throbbing in his head hurt the more he considered the various scenarios, none of which sat well.

And how did Janice fit in? He felt sick that she'd been killed. They had broken up a year ago, after he'd found her in bed with another guy, Simon Wylan, also a firefighter. But that seemed to be a weak motive to set him up for murder.

"Well?" Dana demanded, looking madder than a queen bee.

"Yes, I'm afraid it is possible he could track you down. And that's a risk I'm not willing to take." He reached out to lightly touch her arm. She was still wearing a pair of bright green scrubs, the color matching her eyes, topped with a thin scrub jacket that was white and decorated with shamrocks. "Please, Dana. I need you to go along with me on this. We'll get adjoining rooms. I just need a little time."

"Time for what?" she asked, her voice brittle. She didn't look toward him at all, but kept her gaze focused on the road.

He hesitated, considered how to best encourage

her to go along with his plan. "Time to make sure that you're safe."

There was a long pause as a full minute went by. Then another.

Finally she let out a heavy sigh. "Fine. I'll agree to this crazy madness for now. But not one second longer than necessary, understand?"

"I do. Thank you." He dropped his hand from her arm, relieved that he didn't have to fight with her anymore. "Do you know where The American Lodge is? I know the owner—he's a retired firefighter and a friend of mine."

"Yes." She didn't say anything more and he didn't push her. Right now, he was satisfied to have a destination in mind.

Mitch put his hand to his neck in an attempt to assess the damage he'd done to the wound. It throbbed painfully, as did the lump on his head.

"Don't touch it," Dana said, her sharp tone making him quickly drop his hand. "Check inside the glove compartment, I have tissues and hand sanitizer in there. We'll take them inside with us so I can clean up that incision."

He found the items and set them in the empty cup holder in the console between them.

Ten minutes later, Dana pulled into the parking lot of The American Lodge. He slid out of the passenger seat, wishing there was a way to hide the bloodstained shirt he was wearing. Thankfully, The American Lodge was used to dealing with the Callahans; in fact, Matt had recently paid for extensive repairs several months ago, which had given them extra brownie points. The damage hadn't been entirely his brother's fault, but they'd pooled their money to pay for it anyway. So when he presented himself at the front desk, the woman behind the counter didn't give him any trouble, obviously recognizing his name. She took his offered cash and slid two plastic key cards across the counter.

"Thanks." Mitch walked back outside and found Dana standing near her compact car, her arms crisscrossed over her chest. "Here, you're in room three. I'll be next door in room four."

She took the card, slipped it into the pocket of her scrub jacket and got back in behind the wheel. He reached in to take the tissues and sanitizer, then walked over to the motel door, leaving her to park the car.

He unlocked his side of the connecting door and then sat down in a chair at the small table to wait. A few minutes later, Dana unlocked her side and stepped through the opening, carrying an ice bucket full of warm water and towels tucked under her arm.

"I need to cut part of your T-shirt collar out of the way," she said, pulling a pair of bandage scissors out of her pocket. He wondered what else she had in there and counted his blessings that she was a nurse capable of providing care.

"Have at it," he said.

She didn't hesitate, and he found himself mesmerized by the intensity of her green gaze as she worked on him. After cutting away the bloodstained fabric of his shirt around his neckline, she began cleaning the wound. Then she tsk-tsked under her breath.

"Three stitches need to be replaced," she said, taking a step back. "Leaving it open will only increase the risk of infection."

He didn't like it, but nodded. "Okay. Can you do it?"

"Me?" Her eyes widened comically. "Are you crazy?

I need a sterile needle, suture, instruments…" Her voice trailed off. "No."

"Come on, you can improvise. I saw a small sewing kit in your glove compartment," he said. "There's a book of matches in the lobby, too."

She stared at him for a long moment. "You really won't go back to the hospital?"

"No, I can't. It's too dangerous."

She sighed again and tipped her head back to stare at the ceiling, as if she might find answers written there. "You understand the risk of infection? And how much this will hurt? I'll need to clean the area with the sanitizer, which will burn like mad."

"Better pain than infection and death."

Her lips thinned; she was clearly not happy with his suggestion, but then she abruptly turned and went back outside to find the sewing kit and matches.

Another hurdle cleared. But he had no idea how many other barriers he'd have to navigate before getting to the truth of who'd killed Janice and why.

And even more important, who hated him enough to frame him for her murder?

Dana tried not to think too much about what she was about to do as she gathered everything she needed to replace the three sutures in Mitch's incision. How had this happened? How was it that she had ended up here, providing care to Mitch Callahan while he hid from the law? This kind of thing didn't happen to her. Her life was boring—well, other than the variety of patient scenarios she encountered at work.

Oddly enough, her earlier exhaustion had vanished, leaving an unusual sense of exhilaration in its wake. She told herself it was because she was just as crazy as

Mitch for agreeing to his harebrained scheme, but deep down, she knew that wasn't really the source.

The sad truth was that she'd been living by rote. Work, eat, sleep and work. Volunteer at the local food pantry, then go back to repeat the process all over again.

Giving herself a mental shake, she focused on the task at hand. First she used a match to sterilize the needle, then threaded it with black thread. She washed her hands with the antimicrobial solution.

"This is going to burn," she reminded him, before pouring a dollop of hand sanitizer on his neck. Using the tips of her fingers, she cleaned the area around the incision. To Mitch's credit, he held himself perfectly still and didn't utter a sound.

"Okay." She took a deep breath and picked up the needle and thread. She'd learned how to suture in nursing school, during a rotation in the operating room, but that was different. The patients were under general anesthesia and couldn't feel the needle poking through their skin. And nurses didn't place stitches in the ER, doctors did.

She braced her hip against Mitch's chair, taking another couple of deep breaths. For some odd reason she was far too aware of the scent of his skin, something pine beneath the faint smell of smoke.

"Are you okay?" Mitch asked.

He was the patient, asking her if she was okay. Pathetic. Enough of being a wimp about this.

"Fine. It's going to hurt," she said, pressing the tip of the needle against his skin.

He sucked in a breath but didn't move or make any other sound of distress. Sweat beaded at her temples and the room felt impossibly warm. She passed the needle through the other side, then used the thread to pull the edges of his skin together. She tied the knot, cut the thread with the bandage scissors and released her pent-up breath. "One down, two more to go."

"You're doing great," he encouraged, as if this whole thing was harder on her than it was on him.

"So are you," she murmured. She subtly wiped her temple on the sleeve of her scrub jacket, wishing there was a way to do this without hurting him. There wasn't, so she resolutely picked up the needle again and went back to work. This time, she tried to keep going steadily along, figuring that the sooner she repaired the wound, the sooner she could stop hurting him and the sooner he'd feel better.

"There! All finished," she said, clipping the thread to the last suture. "Just let me clean it up one more time, okay?"

"You're the boss."

That brought forth a rusty chuckle. "Not hardly. No one has ever called me that before."

When she finished cleaning the area around the incision, she stepped back and surveyed her handiwork. It wouldn't win any prizes for being pretty; her sutures were big and clumsy next to the neat ones that Dr. Crowley had placed.

But they'd hold, which was all that mattered. Now, if only she had some oral antibiotics to give him…

"Thank you," Mitch said in a low, husky voice. "I appreciate your expertise."

"You're welcome," she said, surprised at the lump that had risen in the back of her throat. Why was she getting all emotional about this? She looked into Mitch's blue eyes and tension shimmered between them, making her hyperaware of him.

What was wrong with her? She broke away from

his mesmerizing gaze and reached out to begin cleaning up the mess. But Mitch reached out and captured her hands in his.

"I mean it, Dana," he said. "I feel terrible about how you've been dragged into this. I wish there was something I could do to make it up to you."

She stared at their joined hands. His grasp was warm, his skin tanned by the summer sun a striking contrast to her pale fingers.

"I—I have to go." She pulled her hands from his and turned so quickly she almost plowed face-first into the television perched on the top of a low dresser. "Good night," she managed, as she rushed through the doorway of their connecting rooms, closing her side and locking it behind her.

Safe at last, she leaned back against the door and put a hand over her racing heart. She felt breathless and dizzy, as if she'd run a marathon rather than briefly holding hands with Mitch Callahan.

No, they hadn't been holding hands. She tipped her head back, thudding it against the door as if to knock some sense into her brain. He'd been thanking her, that's all. Apologizing for her being attacked at the hospital.

She needed to pull herself together. She'd loved and lost Kent and their baby. She was not going down that path again.

And especially not with a guy like Mitch, with ties to the firefighting community. Loving people who put their lives on the line each day wasn't for her.

With resolute determination, she pushed herself away from the door and made her way into the bathroom. First thing tomorrow, she was going home.

Mitch was a threat to her emotional equilibrium. She needed to return to the mundane routine of her life. And stay far, far away from Mitch Callahan.

THREE

Mitch groaned when he heard Dana's side of the connecting door slam shut followed by the unmistakable click of the dead bolt shooting into place.

What was the matter with him? Dana might have come over to his ER room to thank him, but that didn't mean she liked him.

In fact, dragging her into his mess likely made her dislike him even more. And it was understandable. He had failed her husband and placed her in danger. He absolutely needed to ensure her safety.

But how?

The throbbing in his temples pulsed along with the ache in his neck. He pushed himself upright and went into the bathroom to wash up. His reflection in the mirror made him grimace.

His skin was streaked with black soot mixed with blood. His looks alone could have scared her away. Craning his head to the right, he checked out the incision. It looked good, although he would have given a lot for a bottle of ibuprofen.

After washing away the grime while steering clear of the incision, he went over to stretch out on the bed. He needed some sort of action plan because clearly Dana wasn't going to stick around for long.

The thought of her driving away tonight had him lunging back to his feet. He crossed over and parted the curtains over the window so he could look out at the parking lot. Her car was still there, but for how long?

He was tempted to go out and remove the distributor cap so she couldn't leave. The thought of her heading home and being found by the knife-wielding man made him feel sick.

Yet there was also the possibility that they might need to leave here in a hurry.

No, disabling the car was out of the question. He'd just have to trust that Dana would stay until morning, the way she'd promised.

He let the drapes fall back into place and moved away. Unfortunately, women didn't necessarily keep their promises. At least, Janice hadn't. When he had caught her with Simon, he'd been shocked, appalled and hurt. The only good news about the whole thing was that he had found out the truth before he'd asked her to marry him.

Old news, he reminded himself. He might not understand why she had bothered stringing him along, but it didn't matter. Just because his brothers and his sister seemed to have been bitten by the lovebug didn't mean he had to follow in their footsteps.

Although the idea of being a loner like his brother Mike didn't sit well, either. Regardless, he had bigger issues to worry about. Janice might not have been faithful, but she certainly hadn't deserved to die.

And how on earth could his attacker have gotten into his boss's office to use his phone? He just couldn't wrap his mind around the idea that Rick Nelson had set him up deliberately. With Jeff gone, Mitch was the only fire investigator on staff, at least until Rick found a replacement. Word on the street was that several former firefighters had applied for the job, Mitch's old buddy Paul Roscoe being one of them. In fact, Paul had asked him for a reference, which he'd gladly given.

Questions whirled around in his mind until he fell into a troubled doze. Every creak and muffled thump from other motel guests woke him up, making him go still while staring through the darkness.

By the time morning had dawned, he had given up trying to sleep and dragged himself upright. He went over to see if Dana's car was still there and was relieved when he saw the compact vehicle.

She hadn't left yet. He wanted a shower, but knew he couldn't get the stitches wet. Instead, he made a cup of coffee in the small coffee maker.

As he sipped from the cup, he tried to think of a way to assure that Dana would be safe returning to her home. He'd rather she didn't go back there, at least not right away. Could he convince her to go to her in-laws? Maybe. He remembered how Kent's parents had stood by her during the funeral. Surely they'd stayed close over the years.

If not her in-laws, then maybe some other friend. Someone who wouldn't mind a houseguest for a couple of days.

A male friend? He inwardly grimaced, then realized he was being ridiculous. Why wouldn't she be dating? She hadn't mentioned having a boyfriend, but it wouldn't be surprising if she was seeing someone. Kent had been gone three years.

Yet the way she'd gone pale when he'd taken her hands in his gave him the impression that she hadn't moved on with her life. The idea that she might have shut herself off from men made him feel guilty all over again.

If only he could go back to that fateful night. He had had his doubts about Kent Petrie coming along on the call so soon after his training. Mitch had asked Paul for his opinion, and his buddy had thought Kent would be okay. Mitch had tried one last time to convince Kent to stay with the truck and man the hose, but the rookie hadn't wanted to be kept out of the action. So Mitch had reluctantly agreed to let him take a flanker position, thinking if he kept the rookie close, he'd be able to keep an eye on him.

Only the fire had gotten out of hand really fast. There had been flammable material of some sort stored in a remote corner of the building that suddenly blew up with a ferocious roar, turning the fire directly toward them. Kent had freaked out a bit, clawing at his face mask, and that was when Mitch had realized the seal wasn't tight enough and smoke was seeping up inside the mask, clogging Kent's nose, mouth and eyes.

When Kent had collapsed, Mitch had tossed the kid over his shoulder and gotten him out of there as fast as humanly possible. But it had still taken much longer than he'd expected. The fire was so intense, he'd felt the breath of the dragon searing him from behind.

By the time he had gotten Kent outside and begun CPR, he'd known it was already too late. But he'd refused to stop, continuing to pump the young man's chest in a fifteen-stroke rhythm while a paramedic on scene tried to force oxygen into his smoke-damaged lungs.

Kent had been declared dead thirty minutes later at barely twenty-three years old.

Yet Dana had come over to *thank* him. And what had he done in return?

Drawn her smack-dab into the middle of danger.

He was so lost in his thoughts, his coffee had grown cold. He forced it down and prepared to make a second cup. He briefly considered reaching out to Paul for help, but decided it wasn't a good idea to put his buddy in danger, as well. When his coffee had finished brewing, he heard the sounds of Dana moving around next door.

Maybe he could hire his brother Mike, the only Callahan sibling to refuse to follow their father's wishes of choosing careers that served the community. Mike ran his own private investigator business, and it was possible that he'd agree to watch over Dana for a while, until Mitch could be sure their assailant hadn't used her license plate number to obtain her home address.

He and Mike had grown closer lately, partially because Mike was the only other Callahan who wasn't married and popping out kids. As single guys, they'd banded together. Not that Mitch didn't love his family, because he did. But their weekly Sunday brunches had gotten exponentially more crowded since three of his brothers and his sister had all fallen in love and gotten married.

He had imagined he'd go down that same path with Janice, and when that plan had crashed and burned, he decided Mike was right. Staying single was a lot easier than being in a relationship.

He pulled out his cell phone—the screen was cracked, but it still worked—and put in a call to his brother. Mike didn't answer, so he left a message briefly explaining the events from last night and outlining his plan to hire him to watch over Dana.

When he disconnected from the call, he felt better

having at least the semblance of a plan. Not perfect, but not terrible, either. Once he knew Dana was safe, he'd get in touch with Miles to let him know about Janice Valencia's murder and the attempt to frame him.

The door between their connecting rooms opened and Dana hovered in the doorway, looking beautiful and fresh, as if she'd enjoyed a good night's sleep. Too bad he couldn't say the same.

"Would you like me to drop you off somewhere on my way home?" she asked, sipping from her own cup of coffee.

The fact that she was telling him her plans, not asking, was no surprise. He had anticipated something like this. And her offer to give him a ride was more than he'd dared to hope for.

"Yes, that would be great." He approached cautiously, sipping his coffee and keeping an easy smile on his face. "I appreciate the offer."

"I'd like to get going in the next fifteen minutes or so, if that's okay." She didn't meet his gaze and he felt bad that he'd crossed some sort of invisible line last night. Making her feel uncomfortable was the last thing he'd wanted to do.

"Fine with me."

"Good." She stepped back and turned away. Moments later, he heard the door to her motel room open and close.

He quickly finished his coffee and joined her outside. It looked to be another nice summer day, and he wondered if she was scheduled to work again later that afternoon.

Dana didn't say much as she slid in behind the wheel. He folded his large frame into the passenger seat, slid-

ing the seat back as far as it would go so he had more
leg room.

Once they were back on the highway, she turned to
glance at him. "Do you want me to drop you off at the
hospital so you can pick up your car? You should probably see the doctor again anyway. You need a course
of antibiotics."

"No, thanks. I'd like to check out your place, make
sure it's safe before I leave you there alone."

She frowned, obviously annoyed, and her fingers
tightened on the steering wheel. "That's not necessary."

"It is to me," he said in a firm tone. If she insisted
on taking him to the hospital, he'd lose precious time
finding her address and then heading over to her house.
And what if Mike hadn't gotten his message yet? Mitch
couldn't stand the thought of her being alone and vulnerable.

"I'll take you to the hospital," she stubbornly repeated. "I'm sure that guy didn't get my license plate
number. It was dark and he was chasing us—I doubt
he was able to memorize it that quickly."

He hoped and prayed she was right. "Please humor
me," he said in a low voice. "It's bad enough that you
had to help me escape. Please let me be sure you're safe.
Once I know that your house is clear, I'll go away and
you'll never hear from me again."

There was a long pause before she gave a curt nod.
"Fine."

He let out his breath in a soundless sigh. "Thank
you."

She didn't say anything more, but headed home. He
recognized the neighborhood, a little surprised she and
Kent were able to afford a house there. It was high-class,
full of newly built homes on streets named after vari-

ous birds. He knew what a rookie firefighter's salary was, and while a nurse likely did pretty well, he was still surprised to see the home that was more than twice the size of his modest place.

"Wow," he said when she pulled up in front of the garage. "You have a really nice home."

She scowled. "Yeah. It's big all right."

He raised an eyebrow at her less-than-enthusiastic response. "Let me go in first, okay?"

She rolled her eyes and slid out from behind the wheel. "It's not like you're armed. What are you going to do if someone is here?"

Good point. "Do me a favor and stay in the car while I make sure the house is empty."

"Use the code on the garage to get in. It's 7272." She slid back in behind the wheel and put the keys in the ignition.

He entered through the garage, staying off to one side as the door rolled upward. The garage was clean and mostly empty except for a few bins that were labeled as Christmas decorations.

No one was in there, so he made his way to the door leading into the house. He opened it as softly as possible and eased his way inside.

The garage door led into a spacious laundry room and from there, into the kitchen. The kitchen faced the spacious backyard through a set of patio doors. He moved silently through Dana's house, looking for any sign that someone might have been there. The windows were all closed up tight, the air cool from the central air-conditioning. He preferred fresh air, but in this case he was glad she had kept everything closed up. Made it safer for her in the long run.

He didn't find anything out of place. In fact the

kitchen, living room and guest bedrooms were almost obsessively neat and tidy. Was that Dana's doing? Must be, since it didn't appear that she shared the place with anyone else.

The house was big so it took him a while to clear it. And when he came to the master suite, he felt like he was violating her personal space, opening up her closets, looking under her bed and checking the shower stall.

When he returned to the garage a good fifteen minutes later, he found that Dana had already parked inside and was standing next to her vehicle, resting one hand on her purse, as she tapped her foot impatiently on the cement.

"Everything is clear," he said. "Thanks for giving me time to check it out. Makes me feel better to know you're safe."

She straightened and nodded. "Okay, but how are you going to get back to your car?"

"I'll walk, it's not that far, just a couple of miles. It will give me time to think." He wanted to take her hand in his, but forced himself to stay back. Touching her had upset her before; he didn't want to make the same mistake again. "Thanks again for all your help." He turned to walk down the driveway.

"Mitch, wait." Dana's voice stopped him and he glanced at her over her shoulder. "I'll drive you to the hospital. No reason for you to walk."

"No need, I'd rather you stay home, where it's safe." He wondered where in the world Mike was. Glancing down at his phone, he didn't see a response via text. Sometimes when Mike was on a stakeout, he turned off the volume on his phone, but he should have seen Mitch's attempt to call by now.

"You're being ridiculous," Dana said, her voice sharp with temper. Maybe she hadn't gotten a good night's sleep, either. "I'm not in danger, you are. Yet you want to stroll down the street in the daylight for anyone to see you? Maybe you sustained a head injury because that's the only excuse I can see for your lack of reason."

"Having you stay here safe and sound is perfectly reasonable," he countered.

Come on, Mike, where are you?

When Dana moved to get back into her car, he came rushing back up the driveway. "Okay, how about this? You go inside and I'll hang around in the garage for a little bit. I'll call my brother for a ride."

She paused, nodded, then slammed the driver's-side door shut. "Okay. I guess that will work."

"Great. I promise I'll be out of your hair soon."

For the first time that morning the corner of her mouth tipped up in the barest hint of a smile. "Yeah, why do I find that so hard to believe?"

Dana was so beautiful, especially when she smiled. Yet he sensed she hadn't been very happy over the past few years. Why had it been so hard for her to move past Kent's death? Losing a spouse was horrible, but three years also seemed like a long time.

He tucked his hands in the back pockets of his jeans, more to keep himself from reaching for her than anything else.

"Thanks again," he said as she walked into the house.

"You're welcome, again," she said before letting the door close behind her.

He pulled out his phone and checked for a response from Mike.

Nothing.

He stared at the quiet suburban street. Dana's house

was on Cardinal Avenue, and the lots were spacious, easily a half acre or more, providing a nice cushion of space between neighbors. Where was everyone? It was almost eight o'clock in the morning. Either these people had already headed off to work or they were enjoying a leisurely Thursday, sitting indoors. But where were the kids? It was summer, shouldn't they already be outside playing?

The quiet stillness of the neighborhood was a bit eerie. A little too Stepford-like for his taste. It made him wonder why on earth Dana continued to live here in the house she'd shared with Kent.

Whoa, why did he care? Dana Petrie's personal life wasn't his business. His only responsibility was to keep her safe from harm.

He looked at his phone again. Maybe it was time to call Miles. His other brother should be up by now, and he could really use Miles's advice on how to handle Janice's murder.

Especially as he had been set up to be the primary suspect. Sure, he had gotten out of there before the police arrived, but thanks to the beam hitting him, he'd left his blood behind at the crime scene.

Possibly fingerprints, too, from when he'd gone over to check on Janice. It was only a matter of time before the cops came looking for him.

The image of his former girlfriend lying in the rubble was burned into his memory. Even though their relationship had ended badly, he'd never wished her any harm. Certainly nothing like a bullet to the chest.

One thing he had learned from Miles was that when a woman was found murdered, the initial suspect was always her boyfriend, fiancé or husband. He wondered if she had still been seeing Simon Wylan, and if so, where he'd been last night. If Simon had killed Janice in a fit of anger, it wasn't a stretch to figure the best way to push the blame somewhere else was to implicate the former boyfriend.

It was even possible that Simon could have found some excuse to get inside the fire chief's office. Yep, the more he thought about it, the more it made sense that somehow Wylan was the mastermind behind this.

If only he'd gotten a better look at the guy during the scuffle in the ER. But with the mask hiding the guy's face and the fog in his brain from being hit on the head, he hadn't gotten a clear view. There had been something familiar, though, so maybe it had been Simon after all.

His phone rang, jarring him from his thoughts. Mike, finally. He pushed the button and brought the phone to his ear. "Hey, I need a lift."

"I'm on my way. I just got your message. What's going on?" Mike demanded.

Mitch winced. "Long story. I'll work with Miles to get my name cleared, but I also need you to help me keep an eye on Dana Petrie, an ER nurse who helped me escape. I'm worried the guy who attacked me will come after her."

"I should be there in five to ten minutes tops," Mike assured him. "And you probably won't be able to get in touch with Miles—he's been up all night working the murder scene at the burned warehouse."

Mitch closed his eyes against a wave of frustration. That wasn't good news. There was no way he could put his brother in a position of sheltering a suspect.

He needed a plan B. "Okay, I'll figure something out later. But I still need a ride. And someone to watch over Dana."

"See you soon," Mike said.

Mitch counted minutes in his head as he stared out at the road. He straightened when he noticed a large black truck with tinted windows rolling slowly down the street. It stopped at the intersection and then made the right turn onto Cardinal. The tiny hairs on the back of his neck rose in alarm and he quickly hit the button to close the garage door.

The door slowly cranked down. Not good enough. He barreled into the house, startling Dana badly enough that she dropped a plate heaping with scrambled eggs, too many for one person.

In a tiny corner of his mind, he was touched she'd cooked for him, but there wasn't any time to savor the moment. "We gotta go. Out the back, now!"

"What?"

"Hurry!" He nudged her toward the patio doors, but she resisted, grabbing her purse before going along with him. He unlocked and opened the door that lead into the backyard. He heard the sound of the truck engine abruptly stopping.

"Run!" He pushed her ahead of him so that he could protect her from behind. She had changed clothes and wore a green blouse and faded blue jeans. She took off running through the backyard, her purse bouncing against her shoulder as she dodged between a pair of large trees. He liked the way she was finding cover and followed close on her heels.

Dana zigged right, and he felt something whizz past him. It took a minute for him to see the dart lodged in the side of Dana's purse.

What in the world was going on? Why was the guy in the black truck shooting at them with a tranquilizer gun? Mitch didn't like how he'd gotten so close to hitting Dana. He plucked the dart from her bag and slid it into his back pocket. Then he latched onto her arm, making sure to follow her more closely, urging her to continue taking twists and turns.

After several minutes of running through people's yards, they found a small squat shed. She stopped for a moment to catch her breath, and he used the time to call Mike.

"Change of plans, the bad guy showed up at Dana's. We'll meet you at the corner of Robin and Wren, understand?"

"Got it."

He slid his phone back into his pocket and looked at Dana, whose green eyes were wide with fear. "My brother will meet up with us. I promise we'll keep you safe."

She swallowed hard, tears welling in her eyes, wrenching his heart. He silently prayed for God to keep them safe, but for some reason, praying didn't alleviate his guilt.

He'd done this. He'd put her in danger.

And he had no idea how to fix it.

FOUR

Dana swiped at her eyes, horrified by the fact that Mitch had been right about her being in danger, too. Her obstinate refusal to go along with his plan had almost gotten them both killed.

Why had she been so stubborn?

"I'm sorry, Dana." Mitch's low voice was full of regret. "I know this entire situation is because of me, and I promise I'll find a way to keep you safe from harm."

She sniffled and tried to smile. "It's not your fault, Mitch. You told me I was in danger, but I didn't listen. And without you, I don't know if I would have been able to escape unharmed."

He grimaced and shook his head. "You wouldn't be in danger at all if it wasn't for me."

Maybe, but that wasn't the point. Before she could say anything more, she saw a black SUV turn the corner of Wren Street. She tensed. Had the knife guy found them?

"There's Mike now. Let's go." Mitch put his hand under her elbow and urged her forward. "Heads up, we're both going into the back seat, okay?"

She thought it was strange, but nodded and crossed the distance as quickly as possible. They made it to the vehicle without incident. Mitch opened the back passenger door and waited until she slid across before joining her. The moment Mitch closed the door, Mike hit the gas.

"Thanks, Mike, I owe you one," Mitch said.

"Nah, you'd do the same for me. But you both need to stay as low in your seats as possible to minimize the chance of anyone seeing you."

Understanding that this was why Mitch had decided to sit in the back with her, Dana secured her seat belt and then slouched in the corner between the seat and the door. She wasn't very tall, so it was easy for her to stay low.

Mitch, on the other hand, wasn't short. He tried to crouch down in his seat but couldn't get low enough with the seat belt in place. So he unclasped it and knelt on the floor. She could tell the position he was in tugged at the sutures along his neck.

The nursing part of her brain wanted to protest. What if he pulled out the sutures? But that possibility, along with riding in a car without wearing a seat belt, were the least of their worries.

What would have happened if she hadn't gone over to thank Mitch in the ER? Would the knife guy have caught him unaware and succeeded in silencing him, forever?

Deep down, knowing Mitch was in danger and being framed for murder bothered her immensely. Which was strange, because she hadn't let herself care about others, outside her patients, of course, for a long time. She had held herself aloof from friendships and relationships. Being civil, but never allowing anyone to get close.

At this moment, she felt closer to Mitch than she'd felt to some of her coworkers in the hospital.

"Mike, this is Dana Petrie. Dana, my private investigator brother, Mike Callahan."

Mike's green eyes met hers in the rearview mirror. "Sorry to meet you under these circumstances," he said in a somber tone.

"Same here. Thanks for coming to our rescue," she added.

"Have to say, unlike our other brothers, this is the first time Mitch has gotten himself into trouble. He's normally the good guy." Mike wore his chocolate-brown hair long, dark strands flopping down over his forehead.

"That's because I am a good guy," Mitch said.

"Yeah, well, there's a dead body at the warehouse that is being tagged with your name as the perp," Mike pointed out. "Good guy reputation or not, you're in deep trouble, bro. We need a place for you and Dana to lie low for a while."

The easy camaraderie between the brothers made her smile in spite of the danger. As an only child, she'd often watched large families with a feeling of envy. In a way, it was surprising that she had married Kent, who also happened to be an only child.

For a moment, the memory of how she'd lost their unborn child crowded into her mind. She pushed the memories away with an effort.

This was not the time to wallow in the past. Not when they were on the run from men who intended them harm.

"What about Valerie's cabin?" Mitch suggested.

Mike shook his head. "Matt used it not too long ago and the bad guys found him there. The address is on record as part of the crime scene. You need to go somewhere that isn't connected to any Callahans." Mike shrugged then added, "Or to anyone Dana knows."

"I'm not close with anyone anymore except for Kent's parents," Dana said. And Kent's parents were the ones who constantly reached out to her, not the other way around. "My parents are gone and I'm an only child. No worries on my side."

Mitch surprised her by reaching out to touch her hand. "I'm sorry about the loss of your parents."

"Thanks." The warmth of his hands on hers was distracting. "It was a long time ago. I was raised by my grandmother, who died in her sleep right after I graduated from college."

If anything, Mitch's expression turned more sorrowful. "You're not alone anymore, Dana. My brothers and I will protect you."

"I know." And she did. For some odd reason, she trusted Mitch. Maybe because she knew that he had done his best to save Kent's life that fateful night.

Mike cleared his throat to get their attention. "I have a place you'll be able to use. I occasionally work cases with a guy named Hawk. He owns a cabin on Birch Lake."

"Hawk sounds like a nickname. What's his real name?" Mitch asked.

"He legally changed his first name to Hawk, and his last name is Jacobson."

"Have I ever met the guy?"

"Not that I know of. But trust me, he's good. And not many people know we're acquaintances. Hawk keeps a very low profile."

"Not sure how a guy named Hawk manages that, but a cabin sounds perfect. Have you spoken to Miles?" Mitch asked.

"No. I heard the news of the murder come across the scanner."

Dana wondered if all private detectives listened in on police scanners. "Who is the murder victim? It must be someone Mitch knows if he's being framed for the crime."

A long silence hovered in the car, almost like a living, breathing thing. Dana frowned, trying to figure out why her question would cause this type of reaction.

After almost five full minutes, Mitch finally broke the silence. "The murder victim is a woman by the name of Janice Valencia. And yeah, I know her. We—um—dated for a while last year."

Oookayyy. The pang of envy was stupid and juvenile, so she ignored it. "Why would that matter?"

Mitch caught her gaze with his. "Because I broke things off after finding her in bed with another man."

"Oh. I see." She didn't think she did a good job of hiding her surprise, but really, why on earth would any woman cheat on a man like Mitch Callahan? He was handsome, sweet, nice, gainfully employed and considerate. And why was she suddenly so aware of his good points anyway? She dragged her attention back to the issue at hand. "I'm sorry to hear that. Was she cheating with someone you knew?"

Mitch grimaced and dropped his gaze. "Yeah, with another firefighter, someone I never got along with. A guy named Simon Wylan."

She went still, the name hitting her in the chest like a horrible blast from the past.

Simon Wylan had been one of Kent's best friends, to the point that he'd spent a fair amount of time hanging out with them. Simon had treated her like a younger sister.

Suddenly, for some odd reason, being here with Mitch felt like a betrayal to her husband's memory.

* * *

Mitch sensed Dana's withdrawal the moment he said Simon's name. Not surprising. He knew full well the guy had once been close to Dana's husband, Kent Petrie. The guys had trained together.

The thought of Dana thinking the worst made him feel sick to his stomach. Logically, it shouldn't matter, but emotionally, it did.

"I didn't kill her," he said, breaking the silent tension that now shimmered between them. "I wasn't happy to find out that Janice was cheating on me, but not enough to hurt her, much less kill her."

"How did she die?" Mike asked.

Mitch grimaced at the memory. "Gunshot wound to the chest."

"You don't own a gun, do you?"

The topic of fire investigators carrying firearms was often hotly debated. Most cops didn't think it was necessary, always quick to point out that arson investigators weren't law enforcement. Which wasn't exactly true, because Mitch had the authority to arrest a person suspected of arson.

But despite growing up with brothers who went into law enforcement and his own dad, Max Callahan, being the chief of police before he was killed in the line of duty, Mitch had never seen the need to carry a weapon.

The way he had been attacked at the warehouse fire scene proved him wrong. He should have gone along with his brothers' recommendations. Especially since he'd been recently poking around in his father's old murder case. He had blueprints of buildings around the scene of his dad's murder, but hadn't found anything useful.

Not that he'd gotten very far.

"No." Mitch wished they could change the subject, but they couldn't, since the whole point was to figure out who was trying to frame him for Janice's murder. "But that brings up a good point—we need to check and see if Simon had a permit to carry a weapon, although it seems arrogant and stupid that he'd kill Janice with his own gun."

"We can do that," Mike agreed. "But later. I can hear your stomach grumbling from here, so why don't we find a place to eat breakfast? That will give me a chance to call Hawk about the cabin."

"That would be great." He couldn't help remembering the plate of scrambled eggs that he'd caused Dana to drop on the floor. "And I'm going to need the usual supplies, too."

"Yeah, I know. We'll pick up what we need after we eat, on the way to the cabin."

"The usual?" Dana echoed.

"Disposable phones, cash, computer, clothes and toiletries." Mitch rattled the items off in order of importance.

"We need all that?"

"Yeah. Don't look so surprised. We've had some practice going on the run over the past two years. My siblings are magnets for trouble."

"And for falling in love," Mike added in a dour tone.

Since he wasn't close enough to punch Mike in the arm, Mitch closed his eyes and hung his head with an inward groan. Why couldn't his brother keep his opinions to himself? The last thing he wanted was for Dana to think he was interested in some sort of romantic entanglement. He'd caused her enough discomfort crossing the line last night.

"Knock it off," he said in a low growly tone. "You're

scaring Dana. She probably doesn't understand your warped sense of humor."

Thankfully Mike dropped the issue and pulled into the parking lot of a family restaurant that advertised serving breakfast all day. Mike swung around the lot, so he could back into a parking spot not far from the front door.

Mitch unfolded himself from his awkward spot on the floor and gratefully stretched, being careful not to apply too much pressure to his stitches. Bad enough he still had bloodstains on his T-shirt. Hopefully they weren't too obvious against the black cotton.

A server seated them at a table, offering coffee. Both Dana and Mitch simultaneously responded, "Yes, please," making them both smile.

Mike simply nodded and gestured to his cup.

After they placed their order, Mitch took a sip of his coffee and looked at his brother. "I think we should start with Simon. He's the most logical suspect for Janice's murder."

"Besides you?" Mike asked, his expression deadpan.

He cast a furtive glance toward Dana, wishing Mike would knock it off. "You know I'm innocent. But yeah, basically."

"What's your theory?"

He took another deep drink of his coffee, grateful for the surge of caffeine blowing the fuzziness from his mind. "I'm fairly certain Janice didn't die in the warehouse. There wasn't nearly enough blood. My theory is that she and Simon had a fight of some sort, and he killed her. Then he panicked and decided the best way to avoid being caught was to frame someone else for her murder. So he put her in the trunk of his car." He paused, thinking back to last night. "No, his truck. I think he drives a red pickup truck. At the warehouse, he staged the body, then somehow got access to my boss's office phone and called to arrange a meeting with me there. He hid, waiting for me to show, and once I did, hit me with a two-by-four and then called the police."

Dana cupped her mug, her expression sober. He wished he knew what she was thinking, then chided himself for caring.

"When that didn't work, he tried again, finding me in the ER. Only this time, Dana was there to help me escape."

"It's a reasonable theory, except for the guy showing up at Dana's place and chasing after you with a tranquilizer gun."

He frowned. "Yeah, that's where I get stuck, too."

"Tranquilizer gun?" Dana carefully set her mug down. "You mean that guy wasn't shooting bullets?"

"No." He pulled the dart from his back pocket to show it to her. "It's a good thing you had your purse over your shoulder, I pulled this out of your handbag."

Her eyes widened. "What does it mean?"

He shrugged. "The only thing that makes sense is that he didn't want to outright kill us, but wanted to take us alive."

Dana shivered, and he suspected it was all this talk about danger and death that was getting to her. He wanted to reach out to take her hand, but reminded himself that she was off-limits.

"It doesn't make sense," she said.

"There is another possibility," Mike said. "For using the tranq gun, that is."

"Like what?" he asked.

"A tranq gun is quieter than a rifle. You think they wanted to take you alive, but that might have been a temporary measure. I mean, think about it, Janice's death was staged, why not stage your deaths, too? A tranq gun would slow you down. With drugs on board, they could easily stage the scene however they wanted, like say a murder/suicide or something along those lines. Dana lives alone. They could set it up so that you wouldn't be found for hours, days even."

Dana swallowed hard. "Boy, you sure know how to ruin a girl's appetite."

"I'm sorry, Dana." Mitch shot a narrow stare at his brother. "We don't need to talk about this now."

"Yeah, we kind of do," Mike argued. "We need a plan, Mitch, the sooner the better."

"Okay you're right, but there's no reason to get so— descriptive."

"I'm a nurse. I've seen a lot of bad injuries," Dana said. "That's not the problem. It's just, up until now, I was never the one in danger."

"I'm sorry," he repeated, hating the surge of helplessness.

"Please stop apologizing," Dana said. "You're as much of a victim in all of this as I am."

Before he could say anything further, the server approached carrying a large tray laden with plates of food. His stomach growled mercilessly, and he was embarrassed by Dana's amusement.

Once their food had been placed in front of them, Mike folded his hands and raised an eyebrow. Mitch knew his brother was waiting for him to say grace.

He bowed his head. "Dear Lord, we thank You for this food we are about to eat. We also thank You for keeping us safe in Your care and we hope You continue to provide guidance and wisdom as we walk Your chosen path. Amen."

"Amen," Mike echoed.

Dana's voice was the barest hint of a whispered "Amen."

"Dig in," Mitch said, striving to lighten things up. He glanced at Dana, trying to gauge her reaction. He didn't really know much about her, didn't know whether or not she was raised to attend church on a regular basis the way the Callahans had been.

Not that simply attending church was enough. Janice had gone with him on a regular basis, but that hadn't stopped her from cheating on him.

He did his best not to dive into the meal as if he were starving. His brothers constantly teased him about how fast he ate and that was even when he wasn't as hungry as he was right now. But he needn't have worried—Dana proved to be a fast eater, too, and he couldn't help but grin when he noticed that they finished at the exact same time.

"The nurse's motto—eat when you can, because you'll never know when you'll get another chance," Dana said wryly.

"Funny, that's exactly how firefighters think." Mitch was grateful when the server came over to refill their cups.

"Investigators, too." Mike's phone chirped and he pulled it from his pocket and frowned at the screen. "Miles," he said before pushing the button and holding the device to his ear. "Yeah? What's up?"

Mitch couldn't hear Miles's side of the conversation, but the grim expression on Mike's face gave him a hint that the news wasn't good.

"Yeah, I'll let him know. Talk to you later." Mike pressed the End button on the screen and dropped the phone back in his pocket.

"What?" Mitch demanded.

"Miles has been booted off the Janice Valencia homicide case," Mike said with his usual bluntness. "Your blood was found at the scene of the crime, so you are officially their one and only suspect."

"And?" Mitch knew there had to be more.

"Miles has been ordered to find you and arrest you."

The news wasn't entirely unexpected, but left a heavy ache in the center of his chest just the same. "Okay, then. I need you to give me your keys. Dana and I will leave, and you can claim that I stole your car. Just give us a good hour before you call it in."

Mike stared at him. "What are you talking about? I'm not turning you in."

"Listen, Mike, you know as well as I do that this will put a serious dent in Miles's career, and with two kids and a wife to care for, he can't afford to lose his job."

"Miles will be fine once we uncover the truth." Mike looked at their server and made a check-signing motion in the air. "We need to leave and get to work clearing your name."

Mitch didn't want his brothers to get in trouble because of him. But with Dana to protect, he knew he couldn't do this on his own, either.

He could only hope and pray that he wouldn't be the one to drag the Callahan name into the mud, ruining their reputation beyond repair.

FIVE

Watching Mitch and Mike argue about turning Mitch into the police gave Dana a funny feeling in her chest. Going to the authorities made sense, and logically she should be all over it.

But she wasn't. For some unknown reason, she felt safer with Mitch and his brother than with strangers.

Okay, mostly with Mitch.

Another way she was betraying Kent's memory. She told herself that she considered Mitch only a friend, and that she wasn't in the market for anything else, but it was difficult to ignore the strange awareness that accompanied his woodsy scent.

"Are you ready to go?"

Mitch's low husky voice drew her attention from her wayward thoughts. She nodded, drained what was left of her coffee and rose to her feet. "Of course."

Mitch let Mike take the lead. When they were outside, he glanced at his brother. "Last chance. Give me the keys and then call Miles for a ride."

"Knock it off. You know very well that Callahans stick together no matter what." Mike slid behind the wheel, leaving her and Mitch to resume their positions in the back.

"You better add a new vehicle to the list," Mitch said. "Since Miles was told to bring me in, all Callahan-owned vehicles have the potential to be pulled over by cops who are likely to slap cuffs on before asking any questions. A lot of guys, those who weren't fans of our dad, would salivate at the idea of arresting a Callahan."

"I know. When I called Hawk, I asked if we could swap rides. He's game. Oh, yeah, he said the cabin is yours for as long as you need it."

She caught Mitch's gaze on hers and wondered what he was thinking. Probably that he didn't want to be stuck with her for too long.

"Thanks. Appreciate it. But we're both going to need vehicles. Do you have access to something else if I use Hawk's ride?"

"I can rent something without a problem." Mike didn't sound too concerned. "We'll cross that bridge when we come to it. For now, I'm going to drop you guys off at the cabin so I can pick up all your supplies before meeting up with Hawk to swap cars."

"I have some money," she offered.

"Keep your money. We have it covered," Mitch said with a frown. "None of this is your fault, Dana. Bad enough that I'm causing disruption to your life." He paused, then asked, "When are you scheduled to work?"

So much had happened in the past twelve hours, she needed to think back. "Today's Thursday, right? I'm off until Saturday evening. I generally work the three to eleven thirty shift."

Mitch's expression held concern. "I don't know if we'll have this wrapped up by then. Are you going to get in trouble if you call off work?"

"No, but I hate to miss my shift at the food pantry." Mitch looked confused, so she added, "I usually volunteer there on my days off. They're going to wonder where I am if I don't show two days in a row."

"Which pantry?" Mitch asked.

"Home and Harvest in Brookland." It was the one sponsored by the fire station where Kent had worked, and she could tell Mitch easily made the connection.

"Once we get our disposable phones, I need you to call Louise and let her know you're not going to be available for a while."

She should have realized that Mitch would know Louise Becker, the woman who ran the Home and Harvest pantry. She kept forgetting that he'd once worked in the same fire station as Kent and Simon.

"Okay, but she's going to ask questions about where I'm going or what I'm doing."

"Tell her you're taking a few days off to visit some friends," Mitch suggested. "It's not a lie. Mike and I can officially be considered your friends."

"Yes, but..." Her voice trailed off. She didn't want to explain how her taking time off would be viewed by Louise as a monumental step forward. How often had she heard Louise and others suggest it was time to move on with her life? They'd assume she had met someone. A man.

And she had, but not in the way they would think.

"But what?" Mitch asked.

She forced a smile. "Nothing. I'm sure it will be fine." She made a mental note not to mention Mitch's name when she called Louise and tried not to think about how her absence might impact the people who depended on the provisions they stocked each day to feed their families.

"Hey, when we're safely out of danger, we'll make it up to the pantry, okay?"

Mitch's ability to read her thoughts knocked her off balance. She'd loved Kent, but had he ever been as in tune to her thoughts and feelings?

Guilt instantly washed over her for comparing her dead husband to Mitch Callahan. That was hardly fair. Maybe she and Kent had been young when they'd married, but that hadn't lessened her feelings for him. He'd been a good man who would have made a great father.

The way she'd lost Kent and their baby in a few short days had been life-altering. No one would ever truly understand what she'd gone through.

Least of all, Mitch Callahan.

Not that she planned to tell him. The loss of her baby was a painful secret she'd kept deep in her heart for three long, lonely years.

Mitch hated the shadows in Dana's eyes and wished there was something he could do to help.

"Cop alert," Mike said in a clipped tone. "State trooper sitting in the median a mile up ahead. Keep your heads down."

Mitch glanced at Dana, her eyes wide with alarm. He tried to send her a reassuring smile. "We'll be okay."

She unclasped her seat belt and slid down so that she was kneeling across from him on the floor of Mike's SUV. She was so close, he could see the dark pupils in her green eyes and smell the lilac-scented shampoo she'd used on her hair.

"We need a blanket to cover us up," she whispered.

"I don't have one, sorry," Mike responded. "But a guy driving alone shouldn't raise any alarms, so hang tight back there."

Dana curled herself into a small ball, and it took

every ounce of willpower Mitch had not to reach out to take her hands in his.

Instead, he offered up a quick prayer, asking for God to keep them safe.

Silence reigned as Mike drove well within the speed limit past the trooper. Five minutes passed, then ten, but Mitch still didn't move. Living with cops had taught him to respect their cunning ability to sneak up on a suspect. Mike was obviously thinking along the same lines, because he didn't say anything for another long ten minutes.

Mitch was aware of the soreness in his knees from his prolonged position, not to mention the throbbing in his neck, and he knew Dana had to be just as uncomfortable. He really hated the thought that she had to go through all of this because she happened to be in his room when the assailant attempted to silence him, permanently.

Mike put on his blinker and headed off the interstate. Mitch froze, wondering if his brother was being pulled over after all.

"You can relax now," Mike finally said. "I got off the interstate, it's probably best if we take side roads the rest of the way to Hawk's cabin."

Mitch blew out his breath in a heavy sigh. "Sounds good."

Dana raised her head. "The cop is gone?"

"For now." Mitch wasn't about to lie. "Even if we had been pulled over, I would have made sure that the police knew that you and Mike were innocent. I'd take the blame for forcing you to go along with me."

Mike snorted. "No cop is going to believe I'm acting against my will. But you're right, we need to figure out a way to protect Dana from being arrested for harboring a fugitive."

"I can protect myself," Dana said, uncurling from her spot on the floor. She pushed herself up and resumed her seat, clicking her seat belt into place and then slouching in the corner again. Her silky dark hair made her skin look impossibly pale. "The cops would let me go once I explained how you helped protect me from the guy chasing us with a tranquilizer gun."

Mitch had the dart as proof, but little else. He hated to point out that if they returned to Dana's house right now, there would likely be no evidence of a crime there, other than the scrambled egg mess on the floor, which could just as easily be blamed on him.

He shifted his position in a feeble attempt to alleviate the pressure on his kneecaps. The drive seemed to go on forever before the SUV slowed.

"We're here," Mike announced.

Mitch thankfully returned to his seat, rubbing his palms against his knees. There wasn't anything to be done about the throbbing of his incision. Glancing through the passenger-side window, he saw only trees and more trees. Branches scraped the top of Mike's SUV as he navigated what looked more like a walking path than a driveway.

Then he saw the structure, a green building with gold trim, the colors blending in perfectly with the foliage around them. Mike stopped the SUV in a small clearing.

Mitch pushed open his door and then held out a hand to Dana. She hesitated, then slid across the seat and placed her hand in his, accepting his assistance.

"Is there indoor plumbing?" Dana asked, eyeing the place with skepticism.

Mike laughed. "As if I'd dare to bring a woman here

if there wasn't. Yes, there is indoor plumbing, running well water and basic appliances."

Mitch watched as Mike found the key hidden in the corner under the eaves. The interior of the cabin was flooded with light—there weren't any curtains over the windows—and it was a little dusty. Overall, it was nicer than he'd anticipated and he was relieved for Dana's sake.

"Two bedrooms with a bathroom in between." Mike gave them a quick tour. "Hawk said you can help yourself to whatever food is left here, but I can stop for groceries, too."

"Just bring the phones, spare cash and car. We'll get the rest." Mitch spied a computer router in the corner of the living room. "Do you mind leaving your laptop here? I'd like to see what I can find out about Simon."

"Sure." Mike left, then returned with the laptop. He checked his watch. "Give me two hours and I'll be back with the rest of your stuff."

"Okay." Mitch clapped his brother on the shoulder. "Thanks, Mike. I really appreciate this."

Mike nodded, then headed back outside. Mitch watched for a moment as his brother navigated his way back down the driveway, disappearing from view.

He knew he was blessed to have such a great family, brothers and a sister who wouldn't let him down. But he also knew he couldn't depend on their generosity forever.

Unfortunately, the only idea he could come up with was to confront Simon Wylan about Janice's death.

While hoping and praying the guy would somehow implicate himself in her murder.

Mitch's single-minded focus on Simon Wylan bothered Dana a lot. Murder? Really? She understood why

Mitch might hold a grudge against the guy, especially when he pulled up Simon's social media site—she couldn't deny there were several photos of him and a pretty blonde tagged as Janice Valencia.

She was strikingly beautiful in a TV-model kind of way. Beautiful long blond hair, flawless skin, white teeth, perfect figure.

Her stomach twisted as she realized this was the type of woman who Mitch would go for. Someone as different from her as possible.

Then again, the woman had cheated on him, likely breaking his heart.

All the more reason for Dana to keep her distance.

"Who's that guy?" she asked, pointing to a man standing beside Simon.

"Paul Roscoe," Mitch said, his gaze thoughtful. "I didn't realize he was friends with Simon, too. He's applied to be a fire investigator, like me."

"Hmm." Since leaning over Mitch's shoulder made it difficult to ignore his woodsy scent, she moved away, wandering into the kitchen. She checked out the food supplies and started a list, wondering how long they'd have to stay here.

That didn't take long, so she went over to scan the shelf of mysteries Hawk had left behind.

The two hours dragged by slowly. The crunch of tires on leaves and branches indicated Mike had arrived. She set her book aside and looked at the SUV parked there, also black in color but a different style, sleek in design.

She followed Mitch outside. "This is perfect, thanks bro," Mitch said. "I found Simon's address. I'd like to head over there to talk to him."

"Let's get the phones working and charged up first," Mike replied. "Miles gave me a bit of intel, too."

She huffed out a disgruntled breath, annoyed at how the Callahans acted as if she wasn't there.

It took several minutes to charge up the phones enough to get them activated.

"Miles thinks the bullet used on Janice was from a Glock."

Mitch frowned. "Interesting. When I searched for information on Simon, I found that he has a permit to carry a thirty-eight, not a Glock. Could Miles be wrong?"

Mike shrugged. "He said the weapon was discharged at close range, which means the bullet is mush. So yeah, I guess he could be wrong."

"And he verified she wasn't killed at the warehouse, right?"

Mike nodded. "That's right. His boss wants Miles to bring you in, then to work on finding the scene of the crime."

"Figures. Let's talk to Simon. I'd like to know where he was last night."

"We can ask." Mike didn't seem convinced their efforts would be helpful. He knew it was a long shot, but it was worth a try. "You can drop me off before you talk to Simon. He probably shouldn't see us together."

"I know Simon. I'm sure he'll talk to me," Dana volunteered.

Both men looked at her as if she'd sprouted wings. "I think it's best if you stay out of this," Mitch said.

"I disagree," Mike said thoughtfully. "Dana has a good point. She knows Simon, so it's logical she should be the one to approach him."

"Whose side are you on?" Mitch demanded.

"Yours. But let's face it, Simon is more likely to slam the door in your face than talk to you."

Dana held her breath, feeling relieved when Mitch reluctantly nodded. "Okay, fine. But I'm sticking close by, just in case he tries something."

"Wouldn't expect anything less," Mike agreed. He looked at the address of Simon's apartment building. "Oakdale? That's not far from my place. I'll hang around outside as backup, just in case."

"Thanks." Mitch rose to his feet and unplugged the two phones. "Let's go."

"First you might want to change your bloodstained T-shirt and use one of Hawk's baseball caps to help disguise your appearance," Mike said.

Five minutes later, they were back on the road, only this time, Mitch was driving. No one said much as they made their way back toward town, using less-traveled highways again as they had on the way out.

After thirty minutes, Mitch pulled over to the side of the road. "Simon's apartment building is two blocks from here, west on River Run Drive. Keep your phone on you. We'll let you know if we need your assistance."

Mike nodded. "I'll be around, but you won't see me unless there's trouble."

"I know." Mitch nodded as his brother slipped out of the SUV.

Seeing the large apartment complex brought back a rush of memories for Dana. She'd lived there herself before she'd married Kent. The apartments weren't anything special but they weren't terrible, either. At least, not that she remembered.

Looking at them all these years later, she couldn't help but see the signs of wear in the faded, peeling paint and missing shingles from the roof. For some odd reason, seeing where she'd come from only made her more embarrassed to still be living in Kent's house.

She needed to move out, and soon. This time, she wouldn't let Kent's parents guilt her into staying. It was crazy to have a home that large for one single person to live in. A family should be living there, a large family with lots of kids.

The idea of children made her wince.

"Did you change your mind?" Mitch asked. "It's fine if you did. You can stay here while I go in."

"No." She wasn't about to bare her personal life to Mitch. "I was just reminiscing about how I lived here when I was in school." Her smile was wistful. "I was so proud of the fact that I was living on my own."

"I didn't realize you lived here, too. Did Kent?"

She raised an eyebrow. "Kent Petrie live in an apartment building? Are you kidding? He lived at home until we got married, then his parents bought that house for us as a wedding gift."

"Generous of them." Mitch flashed her a broad smile over his shoulder. "If you haven't changed your mind, then let's go."

She slid out of the vehicle, squinting against the bright summer sun.

"Which apartment is he in?" Mitch asked.

"The middle building there, number 309." She led the way up to the front door, wondering how they were going to get past the locked entryway, but there was nothing to worry about—the door lock was broken. She pulled it open, sad to realize the security had fallen away along with the rest of the building's maintenance.

The stairs were directly ahead, so she chose them over the elevator, unwilling to risk getting stuck. On the third floor, she led the way down to the last door on the left.

"Stay back," she told Mitch. "We don't even know if he's here."

He nodded in agreement.

As she approached, a horrible smell assaulted her. Unfortunately, thanks to her nursing background, this wasn't the first time she'd been exposed to this kind of stench. Her steps slowed and she glanced at Mitch. "Something's wrong. Very wrong."

Mitch's expression turned grim, and he flattened himself against the wall next to Simon's door. Using his foot, he pushed against it.

The door swung open and the smell got impossibly worse. Dana covered her nose and mouth with her hand and peered into the apartment.

Simon Wylan was lying on the sofa in a pool of blood and other assorted bodily fluids. He was dead from what looked like a gunshot wound to the chest.

Instead of their prime suspect, Simon was a victim of murder.

SIX

Mitch could hardly believe what he was seeing. Both Janice and Simon were dead? Killed in the exact same way? Set up as if to frame him for a double homicide?

Why?

He couldn't wrap his head around it. None of this made any sense.

Dana looked pale and ill, making him suspect she must be wondering if he really was a murderer after all. Although if he had done this, the last thing he would do is bring her here to see the body.

"Come on," he said, gently pressing his hand into the small of her back. "We need to get out of here."

She nodded, taking one step backward and then another. The smell was so bad in the hallway he knew it would only be a matter of time before someone called the Oakdale police. In fact, he was surprised they hadn't been called before now. Wouldn't the Milwaukee cops have tried to get a statement from Janice's current boyfriend?

Or was it possible they didn't know about her relationship with Simon? No, they had to know, otherwise there would be no motive behind Mitch's supposed actions. Plus pictures of Simon and Janice together had been plastered all over social media.

So why hadn't the police found Simon's body before now?

There wasn't time to comb through the details. "We need to hurry." He kept his voice low so that she was the only one who could hear him. "As soon as we get outside I'll call Mike."

Too late. The sound of police sirens filled the air. He imagined the authorities coming closer, trapping them inside the building. Dana must have heard them, too, because she instantly switched directions, heading back toward Simon's apartment.

Maybe the police knew Simon was dead and waited to see if he'd show up?

"This way." Dana tugged on his arm. "There's a corner stairwell that leads out to the back side of the building to the surface parking lot."

Considering she once lived here, he didn't argue. Dana led him down a dirty stairwell out into the bright sunshine, summer heat radiating off the blacktop parking lot. He came up short when he realized Simon's cherry-red pickup truck was parked there in plain sight.

The sirens were growing louder, but he crossed over to the truck, peering in through the windows to see what, if anything, might be inside. The outside of the vehicle was pristine, clean and buffed to shine, but in stark contrast the inside was a mess, full of empty fast-food containers and dirty clothes. But there was no blood indicating he'd killed Janice. Mitch's gaze settled on a pair of muddy brown work boots. He could tell they had steel tips in the toes, the kind that guys wore while working on construction sites.

But Simon was a firefighter, not a construction

worker. So why would he need steel-reinforced boots? As a fire investigator, Mitch wore them routinely, but that was only because he was always maneuvering through dangerous conditions in burned buildings.

"Call your brother," Dana urged. "The police will be here at any moment."

She was right, so he reluctantly turned away and called Mike. "Simon Wylan is dead."

"I wondered if something had gone wrong when I heard the sirens," Mike said. "You want me to pick up the SUV?"

Mitch hated putting his brother in the middle of his mess. If the cops saw Mike and recognized him as a Callahan, they were likely to detain him. "If you can do it without being seen. If not, we'll find a new plan."

Mike snorted. "Yeah, right. It won't be a problem."

He smiled grimly at his brother's confidence. "We'll make our way through the back parking lot. There's a Gas 'N Go station a few blocks away. Pick us up there."

"Got it." Mike disconnected from the phone.

Mitch took Dana's hand. "We need to keep our heads low."

"Understood."

He tugged on the brim of Hawk's hat and led the way through the parking lots using various cars scattered across the lots for coverage when available. The apartments were set up on angles and the lots appeared to be shared amongst the buildings. Beyond the parking lot was an open field. Some of the weeds were tall enough to reach his waist, but not enough to hide them from view. He picked up the pace, plowing through the weeds, plagued by a sense of urgency.

The sound of police sirens slowly faded away the more distance he managed to put between them. His goal was to make it to the gas station building that butted up against the opposite side of the field.

Finally, they made it. He ducked around the furthest corner, relieved he and Dana were safely out of sight. He gave Dana's hand a quick squeeze before letting go long enough to peek around the corner at the way they'd come.

Thankfully there was no sign of anyone in pursuit. Now that he and Dana were relatively safe, he found himself worrying about his brother. What if the cops pulled up and were already checking out the SUV's license plate number? Looking back, his decision to park only two blocks away seemed stupid.

Why hadn't he parked six blocks away, or more?

"Mitch? Are you all right?"

Dana's concern made him ashamed. He should be the one asking her that question. This was hardly what she'd signed up for when she'd decided to help him escape from the ER.

"I'm fine, but what about you?" His fingers itched to tuck a strand of her dark hair behind her ear. "It seems like all we've done since we met is run and hide."

Her smile was lopsided. "True, but it's not your fault." Her brow puckered in a frown. "I just wish I knew why Simon was murdered."

"You and me both. I'm truly sorry he and Janice are dead, but I promise I had nothing to do with killing them."

"I know you didn't." Dana's faith in him was humbling.

He heard the sound of a car engine and turned around, relieved to see that Mike had in fact made it to the SUV without being caught. "Looks like our ride is here."

"Good." Dana hurried over to the vehicle, sliding into the back seat. Mitch bypassed the front seat to join her, figuring it was best to stay out of sight for a while.

Mike didn't say anything for several minutes, until they were a good ten miles from the apartment building. "You think the same person killed Janice and Simon?"

"That's the only thing that makes sense," Mitch said from his kneeling position.

"Except it doesn't make sense, not really," Dana argued. "I get that someone is trying to frame you, but killing them both and leaving their bodies in two different locations only draws more attention to the crimes."

"Which might be what they're trying to do," Mike argued. "Puts more pressure on the cops to arrest Mitch."

Mitch couldn't disagree. "I can't even imagine why I'm being set up in the first place."

"Could it be related to the warehouse fire you investigated?" Mike asked. "You mentioned having to take over all of Jeff Walker's cases, adding them to your own. Arresting you for a double homicide would bring your ongoing investigation to an abrupt end."

He hated to admit his brother was right. "Yeah, maybe. I could see that being a motive if someone else took over the investigation, someone like my boss or whoever he hires to replace Walker. The evidence might be changed so that the fires could be deemed to be caused by faulty wiring instead. The way the arsonist originally intended."

"We need to know more about those fires," Dana said. "Like who would benefit the most from an accidental blaze."

It was hard to imagine that anyone would benefit from a string of warehouse fires, especially enough to justify murdering two innocent people.

Unless the two people who'd been killed weren't as innocent as he'd originally believed.

Simon's muddy construction boots bothered him. Why would a firefighter have them? They wore fire- and waterproof footgear, not steel-toed construction boots. As far as he knew, Simon hadn't worked any- where else on his off shift. Firefighters worked twenty- four on and forty-eight off, so some did pick up the occasional odd job.

Maybe Simon worked construction on his off days? Didn't seem likely. Construction was often weather de- pendent, which wouldn't work well for a firefighter who had just forty-eight hours off, some of which needed to be spent sleeping. Most firefighters picked up an occa- sional shift for an ambulance crew, rather than a heavy- lifting kind of job like construction.

No, the more likely scenario was that Simon was somehow involved in setting the arson fires in the first place.

A theory that only confused the entire situation, rather than bringing any sort of clarity.

"Where to?" Mike asked, dragging him from his troubled thoughts.

"Your place," Mitch said. "I've inconvenienced you enough. Better for you if Dana and I go it alone for a while."

His brother didn't respond right away, and Mitch's position on the floor was such that he couldn't tell where they were headed.

"There's a rental car agency that's not far from my place," Mike finally said. "I'll get my own set of wheels and meet up with you at the cabin."

"I don't think so," Mitch countered. "Get the rental,

but don't meet up with us. You've helped enough already."

Mike was silent for a moment. "Okay, I can give you some room here, but I need you to stay in touch. Don't do anything rash without talking to me first."

"I won't," Mitch agreed, mostly because he wasn't sure what his next step would be.

How in the world was he going to find a way to clear his name?

Dana should have been scared out of her mind after finding Simon dead, but oddly enough, she wasn't. Being with Mitch Callahan made her feel safe.

Still, she felt bad that Kent's friend was dead. She knew, deep in her bones, that Mitch hadn't murdered anyone, but she could see how the noose of suspicion was tightening around his neck.

Mike stopped the SUV and threw the gearshift into Park. "Stay down for a few minutes yet. I want to be sure they have a vehicle for me before you leave."

"Sure," Mitch agreed.

She was slouched so low, she couldn't see much, but she heard Mike's door open then slam shut. A heavy silence fell between them.

"Are we headed back to the cabin?" she whispered.

Mitch nodded. "Yeah, for now. We can use Mike's computer to see if we can identify who owns the warehouses that have burned down. Although I had already started looking at Jeff's cases and at first glance, I didn't see anything suspicious. I highly doubt they're all owned by the same person."

She could sense Mitch's frustration. "Don't worry, we'll figure it out."

He stared at her for a long moment, his gaze searching hers. "I don't understand why you're not furious with me," he said in a hushed tone. "I've done nothing but put you in danger over and over again."

She'd be lying if she said she liked being in danger, but at the same time, she couldn't deny she'd felt more alive in the past twenty-four hours with Mitch than she had in days. Months.

Years.

Since she'd buried her feelings and zest for life with Kurt and their unborn child.

But she couldn't say that out loud.

"It's not your fault someone tried to stab you in the hospital." She smiled and shrugged. "Helping you find out who is behind these ridiculous attempts to frame you is the best way for me to get my life back."

"I guess you're right. But I want you to know I'll find a way to make it up to you. I feel terrible that you're missing your volunteer hours because of me."

She lightly smacked herself on the forehead. "Rats, I forgot to call Louise."

"You should do that now, before we get back to Hawk's cabin, just in case…" His voice trailed off.

She frowned. "In case what?"

"It's a long shot, but there is a very slight possibility your disposable cell could be traced."

Wasn't the whole point of disposable cell phones the fact that they couldn't be tracked? Then again, what did she know about technology? It wouldn't hurt to follow his lead.

She pulled out her phone and dialed Louise's number by heart. The line rang several times before a rushed voice answered, "Hello?"

"Louise? It's Dana Petrie. I'm sorry but I won't be in for the next few days…" She barely finished her sentence before the manager of Home and Harvest interrupted.

"Dana? Where are you? The police have been here asking questions about you."

"What?" she looked at Mitch in shocked horror. "When?"

"Earlier this morning. They think you're in some sort of danger."

"Hang up," Mitch hissed. "Now!"

She frowned at him and shook her head. "That's ridiculous, Louise. I'm out of town with some friends. No need to worry. If the police return, you tell them I'm fine, okay? I'll keep in touch." She ended the call seconds before Mitch plucked the phone from her hand.

"The police have already been there?" He'd obviously heard Louise's part of the conversation. "They could have a tap on her phone right now."

That possibility hadn't occurred to her, so she held her tongue as he powered the phone off. He looked so upset, she tried to reassure him. "I thought it was better to act as if I were perfectly fine than to alarm Louise by hanging up abruptly. That would only make her think the worst."

Mitch dropped the phone and rubbed his hands over his face. "You're probably right. Who else will she talk to? Kent's parents?"

"Maybe. My in-laws certainly know about my volunteer work." She didn't add how they'd never embraced her decision. In Kent's parents' eyes, she should live in the lap of luxury, doing things like playing golf or tennis at the local country club.

The problem was, golf was boring and she was absolutely horrible at playing tennis. Besides, she didn't see the point of being more involved in the Petrie life-style than she was already.

Crazy as it sounded, volunteering at Home and Harvest had been her secret way of defying them. It wasn't as if they could publicly denounce her working there. Silly now that she looked back at the situation.

Once again, she was faced with the relentless truth that she'd taken a passive role in her own life since Kent's death. Losing her unborn child had sent her emotions into a deep freeze.

It was embarrassing to realize it had taken a crisis like this to make her see the light. It was well past time she broke away from the suffocating presence of Kent's parents to stand on her own two feet.

Mike returned to the SUV. "Coast is clear," he said.

She straightened up, moving from side to side to clear the kinks from her back. Then she unbuckled her seat belt and pushed the car door open.

Mitch unfolded himself from the floor and climbed out the other side. He gave his brother one of those half hugs that men did before sliding behind the wheel.

Sitting up front beside him felt a little odd, but he didn't say anything as he drove away from the car rental place.

"You didn't mention my call with Louise to Mike," she said, breaking the strained silence.

"No." Mitch shrugged, his face set in grim lines. "I didn't want to worry him."

She understood his need to protect his family, but she couldn't help thinking that they weren't going to be able to fight the men who were chasing them without help.

"We'll just keep your phone off for now and use mine, only for emergencies."

She glanced at him with annoyance. "I'm sorry, but

what part of being on the run from men who are trying to kill us isn't an emergency?"

He glanced at her with chagrin. "I know, I'm sorry. Listen, I'm going to head to the cabin to drop you off. Then I'm going to go to my house to pick up my notes and Jeff's related to all the fire investigations."

He was going to leave her alone? No way. "Getting all of the notes you have about the fires is a good idea, but I'm tagging along."

His jaw clenched. "No, you're not."

Two could play this game. "Yes, I am. I'll stay in the car if you prefer, but you need someone nearby in case you run into trouble. Besides, don't you think it's a strong possibility the police have someone watching your house?"

"I know they're watching my place," he said in a terse tone. "Which is one of the reasons why I don't want you anywhere nearby."

She sighed. "What would Mike suggest?"

The corner of his mouth quirked in a smile. "He'd tell me to wait until dark and to take someone along."

"Well, there you have it. I'm glad that's settled."

"Dana." The way he said her name in that low husky voice of his sent goose bumps of awareness rippling over her skin. "I'm trying to protect you. The cops may arrest me, but I can't bear the thought of your being dragged along for aiding and abetting a criminal."

"You're not a criminal." The denial was instinctive, a fact she believed with every ounce of her being. "And I have confidence we'll figure out a way to clear your name."

He reached out and clasped her hand in his. "I don't deserve your unselfish willingness to help me, but know that I've been praying for us to uncover the truth since this nightmare started."

She'd never met anyone who talked about faith and prayer the way Mitch did. She hadn't opened herself to faith or prayer since losing Kent and their unborn child. At the time, she'd felt as if God had abandoned her when she needed Him the most.

But maybe it was time to try again. For Mitch's sake.

"Then I will, too." She stared at their clasped hands, unwilling to break the tenuous connection.

She liked the warmth of his fingers surrounding hers. More than she should.

SEVEN

Mitch didn't like the idea of dragging Dana along with him while he sneaked into his house for the fire-related notes, but he couldn't in good conscience leave her behind. He momentarily tightened his grip around their clasped hands, enjoying the warmth of her fingers around his.

"We'll go later tonight, then," he agreed. "A little after midnight."

"Good." Dana slid her hand from his and he immediately mourned the loss. Telling himself to get over it, he took a circuitous route to the cabin in an effort to be sure no one followed them.

Once they arrived, he set aside the hat and settled in behind the computer, intent on digging into Simon's past. At least Hawk had shared his network password, so they had decent internet access.

Dana sat close beside him so she could see the screen, as well. The lilac scent of her skin was so distracting, he had to read everything twice.

"What are you looking for?" Dana asked as he scrolled through Simon's social media photos.

"Anything that might give me a hint as to why he has muddy work boots in his truck."

"Maybe he was doing construction side jobs for extra cash," Dana suggested. "I wouldn't be surprised—he was jealous of Kent's wealth."

"He was?"

Dana grimaced and nodded. "Kent invited his firefighter friends over all the time. Simon in particular made a lot of comments about how nice it must be to live in the lap of luxury." She put air quotes around *lap of luxury.* "I told Kent to tone it down, but he liked entertaining so he continued to invite the guys over every chance he had. He didn't see it as flaunting his money, but I sensed they did."

"Interesting." He could see how Simon might have harbored a deep resentment of what Kent had been given freely by his parents. "What else do you remember about Simon?"

She looked thoughtful for a moment. "I know he routinely borrowed money from Kent and rarely paid it back. Kent used to complain to me, but that didn't stop him from lending Simon more money when he asked. I think he felt bad for Simon and figured he was helping out a friend."

Mitch had never liked Simon much; the guy was arrogant, even as a rookie. Now, the more he learned about the guy, the less he liked him. Mitch wasn't okay with someone taking advantage of a friendship by borrowing money he didn't intend to pay back. Not that it mattered, since both men were dead. "Do you have any idea how the Petries made all their money?"

She shrugged. "Real estate, I think. They talked about certain apartment and office buildings." She wrinkled her nose. "Simon used to call them slumlords, instead of landlords, which really upset Kent. I'm sure the property they owned was anything but low-income.

The Petries prefer high-class, as you could probably tell by the house they gave us as a wedding gift."

"Yeah, you mentioned that. Quite an impressive wedding gift."

Her expression turned glum. "I know, right? But how do you say no to parents who want the best for their one and only son? I tried to tell them it was too much and that we'd be happy with something smaller, but they wouldn't listen. They insisted we have nothing but the best. And Kent loved the place."

"I can't imagine being an only child. My four brothers and my sister drive me crazy more often than not, but I wouldn't trade them for anything."

"Four brothers?" She looked surprised. "I only know about Mike and Miles."

He scooted his chair back so he could face her. And so he could minimize the effect of her closeness. Trolling through Simon's social media page wasn't giving him much to go on anyway, and he liked talking to Dana. "Marc is the oldest. He's an FBI agent. Second in line is Miles, who is a homicide detective. I'm third in birth order, then Mike. Matthew and Maddy are twins, but Matthew was born first, a fact he relentlessly teases Maddy about, as if a couple of minutes is a big deal."

Dana's eyes were wide with shock and maybe a hint of envy. "Wow, that's incredible. What kind of work are Matthew and Maddy doing?"

"Matt is a K-9 officer and Maddy is an assistant district attorney." He grinned. "She wants to sit on the bench someday as a judge and knowing Maddy? She'll get there."

"So many cops." She tipped her head curiously. "Why did you go the firefighter/fire investigator route?"

He grinned, remembering his father's grimace when

he announced his chosen career path. Not that his dad was truly upset, but cops and firefighters had a long-standing rivalry, usually good-natured, but sometimes not. Each profession felt theirs was superior, which made for interesting dinner conversation. "Our dad, Max Callahan, was the former police chief and he always encouraged us to go into careers that served our community. But I didn't like the thought of being compared to my dad and my older brother Miles and, frankly, I was drawn more toward the medical side of things, so I decided to become a firefighter/paramedic."

She smiled. "I can certainly understand that. But now you're an investigator."

He nodded, then hesitated, not sure how to tell her that losing her husband on his watch had been the impetus to switch his path. To this day he believed the fire that had claimed her husband's life had been set on purpose, although Jeff Walker had deemed otherwise. No sense in creating doubt in Dana's mind, though. He didn't want to upset her any more than necessary. "I guess those investigation genes in the Callahan DNA won out, because soon fighting fires and saving lives wasn't enough. I wanted to play a stronger role in stopping people who set fires on purpose."

"I can see you as a guy who likes solving a puzzle." She averted her gaze. "Losing patients can wear you down over time."

He understood where she was coming from, so he reached over to cradle her hands in his. "Dana, I have the utmost respect for nurses like you, who work hard to save lives every day. I know it must be difficult when patients die, but you have to know you can't save everyone. Doing your best is what counts."

She dipped her head down as if staring at their joined

hands. "I know, but it's not easy to let go. I often find myself second-guessing my decisions."

Was this about her patients? Or her dead husband? Or both? Regardless, he hated the thought of her grieving. He lifted her chin with his index finger so that she was looking at him.

"It helps to remember that everything happens for a reason, it's all part of God's plan. I know it's not easy to understand His way, but He will always be there for you, no matter what."

Her green eyes held the sheen of tears. "I haven't been a good Christian since Kent's death."

The urge to lean in to capture her mouth with his was strong. She was so sweet and adorable. He managed a smile. "That's okay. We all stumble in our faith from time to time. I will admit that it wasn't easy for me to forgive Janice for what she did. In fact, I still struggle at times. God understands your grief and He's still there, waiting for you to return."

"I've never talked about God or faith with anyone before," she said in a low voice.

Not even with her husband? He didn't voice the question, just continued to hold her gaze. "Praying silently and from your heart is wonderful. But you shouldn't be afraid to talk about your faith, either." He grinned and tried to lighten things up. "You should know by now, the Callahans are a noisy bunch who are not afraid to speak up about anything."

"Your family sounds amazing."

The sadness intermixed with longing in her eyes was his undoing. He leaned over and lightly kissed her.

His intent was to offer comfort, but Dana surprised him by returning his kiss, hesitantly at first, then with more confidence. He wanted to haul her off the chair and into his arms, but held back, allowing her to take the lead.

Their kiss was far too brief. Dana broke away and jumped to her feet, looking everywhere but at him. "I'm sorry, this isn't right. Please excuse me." She turned and disappeared into the bathroom, closing the door behind her.

That was the second time he'd crossed the line with her, and the second time he'd chased her away. He pinched the bridge of his nose, silently calling himself an idiot. The last thing he wanted was to make things awkward between them.

Yet he was worried about her. It couldn't be healthy to be grieving for her dead husband three years after his death. But that was her journey to take, not his.

Which meant he needed to focus on keeping their relationship at the friendship level, nothing more.

The last thing he needed or wanted was another woman who would ultimately break his heart.

Dana covered her flaming cheeks with the palms of her hands, mentally berating herself for acting like such an idiot.

It was only a kiss.

Yes, the sad truth was that she hadn't kissed a man since Kent. But that was mainly because of losing her unborn baby and Kent at the same time.

Physically she'd gone on with her life, but emotionally it was all she could do to provide care to her patients. Moving beyond that had seemed impossible. In fact, she hadn't been attracted to anyone in the years since Kent's passing.

Until now.

Until Mitch, a man who'd done his best to save her

husband's life. A man who preferred tall, stunningly beautiful blondes. A man who'd already been betrayed by a woman. She turned on the faucet and sluiced cold water over her face in a pathetic attempt to reduce the redness.

"Get a grip," she whispered to her reflection in the mirror. "You are not a naive girl. So what if he kissed you? Knowing Mitch, he was just trying to make you feel better. Don't make a big deal out of it."

Her pep talk, along with several deep breaths, helped settle her erratic pulse. She knew she was being ridiculous, but deep down, she couldn't deny the fact that she had enjoyed kissing Mitch.

A lot.

Too much.

This weird...*attraction* that seemed to have taken control of her hormones couldn't go anywhere. Even if Mitch was interested, which she felt certain he wasn't, she wasn't ready to go down the path of loving someone again, only to have it all disappear in one fell swoop.

She placed her hand over her lower abdomen. The thought of getting married and starting a family filled her with dread. To this day she didn't know what had caused the miscarriage at sixteen weeks in the first place. Stress after Kent's death? Maybe. Or it could be something physical or genetic. For all she knew, she might be incapable of carrying a child to full term. Her doctor had offered to do testing, but she'd refused. What was the point? She wasn't married anymore or likely to be again.

At least, that was what she had thought. But kissing Mitch had her reconsidering that decision. Maybe it would be better to know...

Enough. She shook her head and drew in another

deep breath. This wasn't the time to be thinking about romance, love or a future husband. None of those things were part of her plan.

The only important goal was to help Mitch clear his name.

Feeling calmer, she emerged from the bathroom to find Mitch back at work on the computer. He glanced over at her, his gaze questioning.

She forced a smile. "It's after one thirty. Are you hungry for lunch? I can check the kitchen, see what our possibilities might be."

"I could eat," he admitted. "But if you'd rather go out somewhere, there's a pizza joint about a mile down the road."

The idea of pizza made her mouth water with anticipation. "I'd love a pizza with the works, but we may need to save that option for dinner."

He shrugged and nodded. "Sounds like a plan. Whatever you'd like is fine with me."

She puttered around in the kitchen, finding several cans of thick hearty beef soup along with a package of oyster crackers, which would be enough for a light lunch.

Afterward, she insisted on checking his neck wound, and was satisfied that it didn't look infected. From there, the rest of the day passed with excruciating slowness. She kept busy cleaning, figuring it was better to keep her distance. Mitch eventually gave up working on the computer, so they passed the time playing cribbage until they were hungry enough to head out for pizza.

They returned to the cabin around eight thirty in the evening. The sun was setting, but the summer sky was still too light to conceal an intruder. She was exhausted and wanted to take a nap, but feared if she did Mitch would go off on his own, leaving her behind.

"We should get some rest," Mitch said as if reading her mind. "I'll set an alarm for midnight."

She grimaced. "Why? So you can leave without me, while I'm sleeping?"

He looked hurt. "Dana, I already told you I won't leave you behind. I wish you would trust me. I haven't lied to you yet and don't plan to start now."

After a long moment of silence, she acquiesced. "Okay, you're right. You haven't given me a reason not to trust you."

His expression was still a bit wounded. "I promise to wake you up at midnight."

"All right." Dana went into the bedroom and stretched out fully clothed on the bed.

Despite her physical exhaustion, random thoughts bounced around in her brain like Ping-Pong balls. Kent, Simon, Mitch, her in-laws, her job—as soon as she shut down one train of thought another popped up.

Finally she tried to follow Mitch's example, praying for the first time since Kent's death.

And slept.

As a firefighter, Mitch had learned to sleep on a dime, a trick that came in handy since you never knew when you'd have the chance to sleep again.

However, memories of Dana's kiss interrupted his sense of peace.

A restless three hours later, Mitch dragged himself out of bed and padded into the bathroom. Once he finished washing up—he heartily wished he could shower—he lightly rapped on Dana's door.

"I'm up," she responded in a cranky voice.

He turned away with a smile. Ten minutes later, she was ready to go, so they headed outside. The three-quarter moon was bright and millions of stars winked in the sky. Here at Hawk's cabin, the stars were far more noticeable than where he lived and he took a few seconds to enjoy the view.

"It's so pretty out here," Dana whispered.

"It is," he agreed. "Ready to do this?"

"Absolutely."

The ride into the city didn't take long because there was little traffic on the highway this time of night. They reached the outskirts of his neighborhood at quarter to one in the morning. He pulled over and considered his options.

Dana lightly touched his arm. "How are we going in?"

"For now, I'm just going to drive past the house." He glanced over at her. "I need you to help me check out the license plates of parked cars anywhere near my place. One or more could belong to the police."

She looked nervous but nodded. "Okay."

He decided to come in from the east, the opposite direction from where Hawk's cabin was located. He hoped and prayed that if there was a cop staked out nearby, he'd find him. If the cop was smart, he or she would be hunkered down low, since a guy sitting behind the wheel would likely be noticed.

He pulled away from the curb and took several side streets so that he approached his house from the east. The first pass he made, he didn't stop, didn't even look at his house, but simply rolled by toward the next block.

From the corner of his eye, he found a midsize sedan, a typical unmarked squad vehicle, parked three houses down from his. He couldn't see much of the guy's profile, so he shifted his gaze to the license plate. He only saw the first three letters, JEY.

"JEY-563, JEY-563, JEY-563," Dana murmured, repeating the sequence until they were burned into his mind.

"Got it," he said. "Thanks."

"Now what?" Dana asked.

He turned the corner and went down the block behind his place, relieved to see there were no parked cars. He fished his phone from his pocket and handed it to her. "I'm calling my brother-in-law, Noah Sinclair. He's a cop on the force and will run the plate for me."

"He must be married to your sister, Maddy," Dana mused.

"Yep, and he used to be Matt's partner, as well." Mitch rattled off the phone number so Dana could enter them in the phone. "Put the call on speaker, okay?"

"Of course." She did as he asked and after three rings, his brother-in-law picked up. "Officer Sinclair."

"Noah, it's Mitch."

"Where are you?" Noah's tone was sharp. "There's a BOLO out for you. Every cop is being told to *Be On The Lookout* for Mitch Callahan."

"I know, and I'm sorry about that, but I didn't hurt anyone."

"Of course you didn't," Noah readily agreed. "But you must know your family is worried. Maddy's been hounding me for news."

"Tell her I'm fine, but right now I need a favor. Run this plate number for me?"

"Sure."

Dana rattled off the letter and number sequence for Noah.

"Belongs to a MPD officer by the name of Calvin Towne."

"Thanks, that's what I thought."

"Be careful, Mitch. There are a lot of cops out there looking for you."

"I know, but I'll be fine. Catch you later." He gave Dana a quick nod, silently telling her to end the call.

"Maybe this isn't a good idea," she said. "If we get caught…"

"We won't." He drove around the block again, then pulled into the driveway of a home owned by an elderly couple, knowing the vehicle would be less conspicuous there.

"I'd like to come with you," Dana said.

He shook his head. "Not happening."

"You need backup. And I'll just follow you anyway."

He sighed, recognizing the stubborn tilt of her chin. "Okay, ready?"

She nodded and slid out of the passenger seat.

"Stay behind me," he whispered, leading the way. He moved quickly, darting between two houses so that he could get into his backyard. The lawns butted up against each other, and the only barrier was a row of lilac bushes. He pushed through them and went up to the back door. Using his key, he entered the house, then stood until his eyes adjusted to the darkness.

Dana waited patiently beside him. "This way," he whispered, moving through the kitchen to the hallway where the bedrooms were located. One was his, one was a guest room and the third and farthest bedroom he used as an office.

He liked keeping paper files along with electronic ones, since he didn't always trust computers or technology. He found his personal notes beneath the file folder of information he'd gathered about his dad's murder, then picked up Jeff's file, tucking them both under his arm. "Let's go."

Dana nodded, following him out into the hallway. Bright headlights shone through the large living room window. Instinctively, he ducked into his bedroom, tugging Dana with him.

They stood in complete silence for a long moment. When his eyes adjusted to the darkness, he noticed the doorway to his closet was open. Weird, he normally didn't do that because the room was small and cramped enough, even when it was closed.

He moved over to the closet, pulling out his phone and using the screen as a flashlight to see inside. Almost instantly he noticed a shoe box lying on the floor, the lid cocked open.

What in the world? It wasn't his. He hadn't purchased any shoes lately. Using the toe of his boot he lifted the lid.

Inside the box was a gun. Not just any gun, but a Glock.

A sick feeling settled in his gut. He had no doubt the weapon was the one used to murder Janice and Simon and that it had been planted there to implicate him.

EIGHT

Dana couldn't believe what she was seeing. There wasn't a single doubt in her mind that Mitch was being framed for murder, but to see the ugly black gun sitting in a shoe box in his closet was surreal. She'd never seen a gun this close, and it seemed glaringly obvious that it had been planted there.

Whoever was behind this setup wasn't playing around.

"What should we do with it?" she whispered.

Mitch glanced up at her. "I'm not sure. If I leave it here, it's only a matter of time until they get a search warrant and find it for themselves. But if I take it, I'll eventually have to confess to tampering with evidence."

"Which is less harmful to you?"

He looked surprised by her question, then pensive. "Taking it seems to be my best option. The only person who knows it's here is the one who left it in the first place. On the other hand, leaving it in a shoe box is a total cliché. Anyone with half a brain would put it someplace safer, so maybe it would be better to leave it behind…"

As a nurse, Dana always trusted her gut, and right now her instincts were screaming, *Take the weapon with you.* She knelt down, replaced the lid and picked up the box. The gun shifted inside with a dull thud. "We're not leaving this here where it can be used against you. Better to ask forgiveness later."

His lips twitched in a smile. "Stay close," he warned, then powered off the light.

She grabbed on to his belt, disconcerted by the abrupt curtain of darkness. Mitch didn't move for several long moments. There was nothing but silence.

He took a few steps forward, and she followed, trying not to step on the back of his heels. When they reached the hallway, the moonlight enabled her to see enough that she could let go of Mitch's belt.

They made their way into the kitchen. The door leading out to the backyard was so close she could touch it.

But a sound at the front door made her freeze.

Someone is out there!

With wide eyes she stared at Mitch, wondering what they should do. Stay and hide? Or get out of there? Mitch swiftly opened the door and gestured for her to go on ahead.

She didn't hesitate, even though she was afraid he'd insist on staying behind. But he didn't. The minute she was through the door, he was behind her, closing the door softly behind them.

She retraced their steps, crossing the lawn toward the lilac bushes. They didn't speak, unwilling to make the slightest noise that might attract attention.

It wasn't until they were out on the street with Hawk's SUV within sight that she felt safe. She ran toward the vehicle, sliding into the front seat at the same moment Mitch crawled in behind the wheel.

Twin beams of headlights blinded them.

The police?

Mitch started the engine and punched the gas. She grabbed her seat belt and jammed it into place. The headlights came straight for them, but Mitch didn't waver. Her heart was lodged in her throat and she feared they'd crash head-on with the other vehicle.

At the last possible second Mitch swerved; the two wheels on her side of the vehicle went down into the ditch, making the SUV tilt crazily for a moment. She let out a squeak of fear, bracing herself on the dash. But then Mitch managed to yank the wheel, bringing the vehicle back up to the level road.

He went straight for several blocks, then turned right, and then left, then right again. She knew he was doing his best to get far away, losing whoever had come upon them.

But if that was the police back there, she figured it was only a matter of time before they caught up, lights flashing and sirens wailing.

"Where should we go?" Her fingers were shaking, so she clenched them together so he wouldn't notice. "Do you think they have Hawk's license plate number now, too?"

"Good question." Mitch's voice was grim and he kept a vigilant eye on the rearview mirror. "I'm thinking we may want to avoid the cabin for now. A motel might be better. But I don't think we can use The American Lodge, it's linked to the Callahan name—not to mention a logical place for a former firefighter to go. We need to find something else. Preferably a small place off the main highway."

"I don't know many hotels or motels," she admitted. "Just the one located a half mile from Trinity Medical Center. We encourage our patients' families to stay there and I think the manager offers them a discount."

"Nice for the patients, but won't work. Whoever is looking for us knows you're a nurse. They'd follow up on any connection to the hospital."

"Okay, then maybe we should head farther south or north, since Hawk's cabin is west of here."

"North," he agreed. "Maybe the Stilton area."

"Works for me."

Mitch took the long way around, going all the way east to the lakefront before turning and heading north. He stayed off the interstate and had to backtrack a few times because of road construction. Ten miles outside of Stilton, she noticed a billboard advertising The Sandpiper Motel.

"How about that one?" she asked.

"Why not?"

The Sandpiper Motel wasn't as pretty or delicate as its namesake. The place was rather run-down, but the red vacancy sign was encouraging. Mitch pulled up to the lobby, shut off the car and turned toward her. "Stay here, okay? I'll get us two rooms."

"Adjoining rooms if possible." She offered a wan smile. "We can work together reviewing your notes."

"I'll see what's available." He slid out and slammed the car door behind him.

She sat back in the seat, fighting an overwhelming surge of exhaustion. Her attempt to nap after dinner had been a complete failure, and she'd been up for more than eighteen hours straight. Peering through her window, she watched as Mitch spoke earnestly to the young woman at the desk in the lobby. He smiled, and Dana felt certain the young woman wouldn't be able to resist his Callahan charm.

And she was right. Mitch returned just a few minutes later carrying two key cards tucked in their respective envelopes. "Adjoining rooms located on the back side of the building."

"Great." She figured he was hoping to keep Hawk's SUV hidden from view back there, just in case the plate number had been tracked down.

She carried the shoe box with the gun into her room, thinking it was probably better than leaving it in the car. She opened her side of the connecting door, then looked around the room, wondering where to hide the box. She'd just finished tucking it into one of the drawers of the nightstand when Mitch opened his side of the connecting door.

"I'm going out for a few minutes. I won't be long."

She tensed. "Where are you going?"

He hesitated. "I'm going to borrow the motel clerk's cell phone to leave a message for Mike. I want him to know what happened, in case Hawk gets a visit from the police."

She grimaced. "Good point. Do you want me to start reviewing your notes while you're gone?"

"Why don't you try to get some rest? We'll have plenty of time to review the notes, and besides, Mike might have some additional information that might help us anyway."

She glanced past him to see the two file folders sitting on the small desk in his room. Was he afraid of what she might find? Or was he simply being nice?

Why was she feeling so suspicious all of a sudden? She trusted Mitch, didn't for one minute believe he'd killed anyone.

"All right." She summoned a smile. "Let me know if you find out anything."

"I will. But please, try to get some sleep." The concern in his eyes made her realize how long it had been since anyone cared about how she was doing. Sure,

Kent's parents often hovered over her, but that felt suffocating.

This was different.

Mitch stared at her for a long moment before he
turned away. She stayed where she was long after the
motel door closed behind him.

Leaving her to wonder how she'd manage to break
through the silken web of feelings she had for him.

Suzy, the motel clerk, popped a wad of gum as she
handed over her cell phone. He'd slipped her an extra
ten bucks to borrow it and she'd jumped at the chance.

He felt years older than Suzy, a college sophomore
who'd explained that she worked nights in the motel
lobby because it was a job that provided her plenty of
time to study.

"Thanks again," he said as he took her phone and
dialed Mike's number. It was two o'clock in the morning, so he wasn't sure his brother would pick up, but
surprisingly he did.

"Hello?" Mike's tone was cautious, no doubt because
he was calling from Suzy's number, with an area code
different from Milwaukee.

"It's Mitch." He glanced at Suzy, who was pretending
to study, so he moved away from the counter. "Sorry to
call so late, but I need you to warn Hawk."

"Why?" Mike's sharp tone made him wince.

"I picked up my notes along with Jeff's files from
my place." He hesitated, unwilling to say too much with
Suzy just a few feet away. "Unfortunately, it's possible
his license plate was identified."

There was a long silence. "Where are you now?"

"Stilton. Motel called The Sandpiper."

"Good. I'll meet up with you tomorrow. Plan to stay for two nights, okay?"

"Sure." There was so much more Mitch wanted to say, but this wasn't the time or place. And he felt bad enough about possibly blowing the cover Mike had worked hard to give him. "See you tomorrow, then."

"Be safe." Mike disconnected from the call.

Typical Mike, not one for small talk. He returned Suzy's phone with a wan smile. "Thanks, appreciate it."

She lifted a bony shoulder. "No problem."

Mitch headed outside, but didn't return to his motel room. Instead he went over to a narrow strip of grass and weeds, searching for enough mud to cover Hawk's license plates. The vehicle was safe enough parked behind the motel, out of view from the street, but what if they had to leave again? Better to cover all his bases than to be caught unawares again.

Too bad he hadn't thought of this trick before sneaking back to his house.

The ground was crumbly, not muddy enough thanks to the lack of rain, so he had to go inside to fill the ice bucket with water in order to complete his task. Afterward, he washed up in the bathroom, then took a moment to peek in on Dana.

She was curled on her side, with her hands tucked beneath her cheek, sound asleep.

Unwilling to disturb her, he ducked back into his room. Remembering how she'd picked up the shoe box with the Glock made him smile. For a woman who had every right to be mad at him for dragging her into danger, she'd turned out to be an amazing partner. She didn't complain or whine—in fact she seemed just as determined as he was to clear his name.

He didn't deserve her support, not after the way he'd

failed to save Kent. But all he could do now was to make sure to keep her safe from harm.

Dropping into a seat at the desk, he yawned and opened the file with his notes. It was late, and the writing tended to blur as his eyelids grew heavy. He pried them open and attempted to concentrate. But after reading the same sentence for the third time, he gave up.

A few hours of sleep, he told himself. Just enough to take the edge off.

He closed his eyes, thought of Dana, smiled and slept.

Morning sunlight streamed through the windows when Dana woke up, groggy and disoriented. It took a moment for her to remember this was a room at The Sandpiper Motel, and that they'd come here instead of heading to Hawk's cabin.

She rolled out of bed, grimacing at how her clothes were wrinkled from sleeping in them, and tiptoed to the connecting door between their rooms. After listening for a moment and hearing nothing but silence, she risked a quick glance.

Mitch was still asleep.

Plenty of time for a shower, even if she didn't have fresh clothes to change into. Twenty minutes later, she felt better—at least her hair was clean. But her stomach rumbled with hunger, as if the pizza they'd shared last night for dinner had been days instead of twelve hours ago.

Flipping through the brochure on the desk, she found a listing of restaurants located nearby, several serving breakfast. She stood in the center of her motel room, debating her options, when she heard movement from

Mitch's room. She sat down and within a few minutes he knocked on the connecting door.

"Come in."

"Hey." Mitch's dark blond hair was damp and he looked amazingly handsome.

"I hope you didn't shower. You're not supposed to get your sutures wet."

"I didn't, just washed my hair in the sink and used a towel around my neck to keep them dry." He had the two file folders tucked under his right arm. "Hungry?"

"Oh, yeah." She jumped to her feet. "There's a Karen's Kitchen just a few blocks up the road. And it's a nice day for a walk."

"Perfect."

After all the sneaking around the previous day, first at Simon's apartment and then in and out of Mitch's house, it felt strange to walk down the sidewalk next to Mitch. Their fingers brushed by accident, and she had to physically stop herself from reaching for his hand.

"Did you talk to Mike?" she asked, breaking the silence.

He nodded. "Told him to warn Hawk about last night. Mike didn't sound happy, but he's planning to head up here sometime this morning."

"Maybe between the three of us reviewing your notes, we'll find something significant."

He sent her a sidelong glance. "I appreciate your support, Dana. You've been great through this nightmare."

Warmth crept into her cheeks at his praise. "I just hate that you're being framed for something you didn't do, that's all."

"I don't take everything you're doing for me for granted." His voice was low and serious.

She wasn't sure how to respond to that, so she simply smiled. How could she explain that she felt alive for the first time in three years? Not because of the danger, though.

Because of Mitch.

Caring about someone other than her patients had brought light and strength to the forefront of her life.

Mitch opened the door of Karen's Kitchen for her. She stepped inside, the enticing scent of coffee, bacon and eggs making her mouth water.

"How about that booth in the corner?" Mitch asked.

"Of course." The hostess picked up two plastic-coated menus and led them to the isolated booth Mitch had requested. Being tucked in the back provided them with a full view of the restaurant and privacy.

A woman close to her own age approached with a pot of coffee. "Good morning, my name is Kathleen and I'll be serving you today."

Kathleen flashed a flirty smile at Mitch, as if Dana wasn't even there. She squelched an unbecoming flash of jealousy and added cream to her coffee.

Once they'd placed their order and Kathleen had disappeared to take care of her other customers, Mitch opened one of the file folders, angling it so that they could both read.

"These are my notes on the most recent warehouse fire. I compared this fire to some of my other cases, but there doesn't seem to be any link."

She nodded, although a lot of the notes were in fire-fighter jargon and meant little more to her than gibberish. "What type of comparisons do you look for?"

"Every fire leaves evidence behind." Mitch's blue gaze grew intense. "The type of accelerant used, the actual mechanism of the fire, those are the details that an arsonist leaves behind, like a murderer's modus operandi. It's the best way to track a serial arsonist."

"Interesting." She was intrigued by the depth of his investigation. "What motivates someone to set fires in the first place?"

"Good question." He smiled like a proud teacher praising a student. "There are many motives. Some firebugs just like to watch things burn, fascinated or obsessed with fire itself. But other arsonists burn for insurance money or even for revenge. That's also a big part of their MO. It's my job to link the clues together to form a big picture."

She could see that his notes included a lot of just that type of detail.

Kathleen approached with their breakfast, so Mitch quickly flipped the folder shut and tucked it away.

Dana picked up her fork, then set it down again when Mitch put his hand out on the table palm up. She tentatively rested her palm against his and bowed her head as he prayed.

"Dear Lord, thank You for this delicious food we are about to eat. Also for keeping us safe in Your care. We ask for Your grace and guidance as we continue this journey for truth. Amen."

"Amen," she echoed. She raised her head, looking directly into Mitch's eyes. "That was a wonderful prayer."

He cocked his head. "Thanks, but all prayers are wonderful. It's our way to talk to God."

"Very true." She dropped her gaze to their joined hands. "I have to admit, I'm still struggling with understanding God's plan for taking Kent so young. But I'm trying. I appreciate you helping to remind me what's really important."

His fingers tightened around hers. "You're welcome."

She reluctantly pulled away from his grasp so he could eat. The food was amazing, or maybe she was exceptionally hungry. She did her best to slow down, but without much success. Mitch laughed when they both sat back, looking askance at their empty plates.

"I don't think I've met anyone who could eat as fast as me," he said.

"Hey, at least we have more time to review your notes."

His smile faded. "Yeah. But I think I should look at Jeff's cases first. After all, this most recent fire was originally assigned to him, not to me. I only got it by default."

"Okay." She cradled her mug, sipping her coffee. "Maybe there's a trend with his fires?"

Mitch waited until Kathleen removed their empty plates, refilled their coffee cups and then left them alone before he opened his own file. Once again, he slanted it so she could see, as well.

Almost instantly the name Shelton jumped out at her. Shelton, Inc. "What's this?" she asked, tapping her fingertip on the name.

"Looks as if a shell corporation by the name of Shelton, Inc. is the real owner of the warehouse. Why?"

A chill snaked down her spine and her mouth went sandpaper dry. "Shelton is Kent's mother's maiden name. Her full name is Alice Shelton Petrie."

Mitch shrugged. "There may not be a connection. After all, Shelton is a fairly common name."

The breakfast she'd eaten swirled in her stomach. Sure, Shelton wasn't an uncommon name, but how many Sheltons had ties to real estate in Wisconsin?

Was it possible there was a link between the arson and Kent's mother's family?

NINE

"Dana? What's wrong?"

She could feel the color draining from her cheeks, and a wave of dizziness washed over her. Mitch leaned closer, his expression full of concern.

"I just—" She hesitated and then slowly shook her head. "Don't you think this is a huge coincidence? Kent's family being in real estate and now Shelton, Inc. owning the warehouse destroyed by arson?"

He reached out and took her hand in his. "Yeah, I see where you're coming from, but think about it. Why would Kent's family be involved in something like this? They're already wealthy, right? And besides, their son was a firefighter. In fact, he died in a fire. It's inconceivable that they were involved."

She frowned, not at all convinced. "But what if they are? I mean, sure, I doubt they meant for Kent to be hurt, but..." Her voice trailed off.

How could she explain the weird dynamics of Kent's family? They behaved as if they were close, but she couldn't help but see it as nothing more than an act put on for the benefit of others.

Specifically for her.

He gently squeezed her hand. "Let's walk back to

the motel where we can talk in private. I'd like to hear more about the Shelton side of the family."

"Okay."

He put the file folders together then gestured for Kathleen to bring the check. Their server sashayed over, favoring him with a broad smile. Dana inwardly rolled her eyes at her flirtatiousness. "Come back and visit again soon."

Mitch seemed oblivious, barely sparing her a glance. "Sure thing." After tossing enough cash for the bill and a tip, he slipped out of the booth. He tucked the file folders beneath his arm, then reached again for Dana's hand. She took it, grateful for the physical connection.

The world suddenly seemed off-kilter, as if nothing made sense. Seeing Shelton, Inc. had been awful. But holding on to Mitch's hand felt right.

She didn't say much during the brief walk back to The Sandpiper. Mitch kept sending her sidelong looks as if expecting her to collapse in a puddle of emotion.

Maybe he was right. She stiffened her spine. The idea that anyone with a firefighter in the family would be a part of purposefully setting fires was ludicrous.

Still, it wasn't easy to shake off the possible connection. It didn't have to be anyone close to Kent's parents who were involved, but a distant member of the Shelton family. Someone coldhearted enough not to care about the impact of arson to a firefighter.

Her heart squeezed in her chest as she thought about the unborn child she'd lost. What if Kent hadn't died in the fire? Would she have been able to carry the baby until full term? Would she have a son or daughter right now?

For a moment her vision blurred, then Mitch's voice

pulled her back to the present. "Looks as if Mike isn't here yet."

Focus. The past was dead and buried in twin graves. She needed to keep moving forward. She cleared her throat. "What time do you think he'll get here?"

"Probably not for another hour yet." He let go of her hand to unlock his motel room door, holding it open for her. "Let's sit here in my room for a few minutes, okay?"

She nodded, dropping into the seat beside his. The rooms weren't large, the two chairs so close that their knees bumped. Mitch set the folders down, then offered an encouraging smile.

"What do you know about the Shelton side of Kent's family?"

She took a deep breath and then let it out slowly. "Kent's mother has two brothers, Darnell and Oliver Shelton."

He nodded. "How old are these guys?"

"Mid- to late-fifties. Kent's parents were already in their late thirties when they had him and they're big on keeping old family names. Kent's full name was Kent-worth Edward Petrie." She waved an impatient hand. "Doesn't matter. The brothers are both older than Alice, by several years if I remember correctly. Kent's mother made a comment about how her brothers were close, but she was the odd person out."

"Oliver and Darnell." Mitch jotted their names down on motel stationery. "Do they have kids?"

"I think so." She cast back in her memory. "Kent had several cousins, but we didn't see them often."

"Anything you can remember might help," he said encouragingly.

It was difficult to imagine Kent's cousins being involved, but she took the pen from Mitch and started with the first names. "Olivia, Archie, Bertrand and Leon. I think Olivia is Oliver's daughter. He wanted a boy to carry on his name, but had to make do. I don't think he had another son, so the other three must belong to Darnell."

"It's a great start." Mitch opened the file folder again, the one holding Jeff's notes. "I'll see if I can find any reference to first names."

She watched Mitch skim through the small, tight script. It took a few minutes for her to realize she was holding her breath, as if afraid of what he might find. Unable to sit still, she rose to her feet and wandered to the window overlooking the narrow parking lot behind the motel. Hawk's SUV was parked there, along with two other cars. The place obviously wasn't filled to capacity.

"I don't believe it." Something in Mitch's voice lifted the hairs on the back of her neck.

"What?" She turned and leaned against the window, in case her knees gave way. "Did you find something?"

Mitch lifted his grim gaze to hers. "The initials *O.S.* handwritten in the margin of Jeff's notes."

"Oliver or Olivia Shelton," she whispered. "That's incredible. Why on earth would Kent's family be involved in something criminal?"

"We don't know that for sure," Mitch countered. "The initials could be related to something else."

They weren't. She knew it and so did he. Her chest felt tight and it was difficult to breathe.

"Dana, don't do this." Mitch was suddenly standing in front of her, his hands cupping her shoulders. At that moment she wanted nothing more than to hide within the shelter of his arms, seeking strength and re-assurance.

"Do what? Believe the worst about the family of the man I married?"

"Exactly that. Not until we have more proof." Mitch's voice was low and tender. "Something more than two letters that could mean anything written in the margin of a notebook."

"It has to be Oliver," she whispered.

"Dana…" Her name came out in a low groan and he pulled her close, cradling her against his chest, the side opposite from where his incision was located.

She clung to him, seeking his strength. His warmth.

He pressed a kiss to her temple, sending a shiver of awareness down her spine. Memories of their previous kiss made her realize how much she wanted to repeat the experience.

Over and over again.

Leaning back in his embrace, she looked into his eyes. His were hesitant and questioning, as if unsure of what she wanted. Likely because of the way she had reacted last night, running away and hiding from him.

But she hadn't been able to hide from herself.

She was attracted to Mitch. He awakened feelings inside her she'd thought were dead, forever. She lifted up on her tiptoes and kissed him.

His mouth instantly responded to hers, deepening the kiss. She reveled in the way he crushed her close as if he'd never let her go, kissing her as if there was no tomorrow.

Dana had no idea how long the embrace would have lasted if a sudden pounding on Mitch's motel room door hadn't caused them to spring apart, both breathless and dazed.

"Mitch? It's me, Mike."

Mitch blew out a heavy breath. "Coming."

She swallowed the insane urge to giggle. He lifted his hand to cup her face, his thumb stroking her cheek. "I'm glad you didn't run away this time. Please know, the last thing I want to do is hurt you."

His sweetness was almost her undoing. She wanted to explain that it wasn't him, but the depth of her own feelings that frightened her.

"Mitch?" Mike pounded on the door again.

Mitch sighed heavily, let her go and crossed over to the door.

Dana stayed where she was, leaning weakly against the wall, realizing just how much she cared about Mitch.

And wondering how she'd manage to live without him once they'd cleared his name.

His brother's timing was lousy. Mitch glared at Mike, wondering why he couldn't have waited just another five minutes.

Or at least long enough for him to tell Dana how much he cared about her.

"Hey, you guys okay?" Mike glanced between Mitch and Dana as if sensing the tension simmering between them.

Mitch sidestepped in front of Dana in an attempt to shelter her from Mike's piercing gaze, one known to see too much. "We, uh—might have a lead on the arson fires."

That news helped divert his brother's attention. "What kind of lead?"

Mitch gestured toward the paperwork on the small desk. "We've been reviewing Jeff Walker's notes. The most recent warehouse that burned was owned by Shelton, Inc. Dana recognized the name."

Mike raised his brow and angled around to look at Dana. "You've heard of them?"

She pushed herself away from the wall and came over to sit at the small desk. "Kent's mother's maiden name is Shelton. And Kent's parents are big into real estate."

Mike let out a low whistle. "Interesting coincidence."

Mitch dragged his gaze from Dana, forcing himself to stay on task. "And that's exactly what it could be, a strange coincidence."

"Yeah, right." Dana pulled the file folder closer and he knew she was looking for the initials *O.S.*

"How does knowing who owned the warehouse help us?" Mike asked. He edged behind Mitch to sit on the side of the bed, leaving the other seat at the table empty. For him.

Subtle, his brother was not.

"I don't know," Mitch admitted. "It might help us figure out who has the most to gain from the loss of a warehouse, but it sure doesn't help identify who hates me enough to frame me for murder."

"Wait!" Dana's head snapped up. "What if we're looking at this backward? What if the guy who burned the warehouse is trying to hurt Shelton, Inc.? The arsonist could be an enemy of Kent's parents."

He had to admit the idea had merit. "Could be. Maybe someone who felt cheated out of some real estate deal. Or someone who is holding some other grudge against them."

Dana looked relieved. Obviously the thought of someone working against Kent's family was more palatable than the other way around. "Maybe I should call them. See if they'll meet with us."

"No way." His instinctive refusal caused her eyes to narrow and he hastened to explain. "We can't do that until we know for sure they're innocent."

She crossed her arms over her chest defensively. "You were the one who mentioned how crazy it would be for Kent's family to be involved in setting fires in the first place. They loved Kent. Their world was destroyed after his death." She leaned forward, her gaze pleading. "We need to talk to them. How else are we going to find out who might have a reason to hurt their business?"

Mike cleared his throat. "I have to side with Mitch on this one. We need more information before we start poking around, looking for skeletons in the closet."

He shot his brother a look of gratitude. "Dana, do you know of anyone who might be upset with the Petries? Or the Sheltons? Think back to family gatherings you've attended over the years. Anything odd stand out?"

Dana sat back in her chair, a tiny frown puckered in her brow. She didn't say anything for a long time, then finally heaved a sigh.

"Nothing sticks out as unusual, although it's not as if Kent's family is very close in general. They don't do backyard cookout kinds of parties, but hold formal events, complete with catered food and hired bartenders and servers." She raised her palms in a gesture of helplessness. "I sometimes had the idea that Kent's father, Edward, didn't get along as well with Oliver or Darnell, but it's more of a feeling rather than anything concrete."

"Ever hear any arguments or disagreements?" he pressed.

"Outside of the underlying tension?" She shrugged. "Not really."

"They probably wouldn't argue or fight around Dana," Mike pointed out. "She was the outsider. Sure, she married their son, but they sound like people who keep up appearances no matter what is going on."

"You're right," Mitch agreed. "Even if the family didn't get along, it won't help us figure out who their enemies might be."

Mike leaped up from his seat. "I almost forgot, I brought a replacement laptop for you guys."

"That should help." Mitch propped the motel room door open, allowing the summer breeze to waft in.

When Mike left them alone, Dana whispered, "Did you tell him about the gun that was planted in your closet?"

He winced. "Not yet."

"Don't you think we should?"

"He's already mad I went back to my place, so I'll fill him in later. Right now, we have other leads to follow."

Mike returned a few minutes later with the laptop. His brother pushed the file folders aside so he could set it on the small table.

Mitch opened the laptop, then crawled beneath the table to plug it in. Dana moved out of her seat so that Mike could sit beside him.

The first thing he did was check social media for photos of Oliver Shelton. "I can find pictures of Olivia, but nothing on Oliver."

"Not surprising. He likes his privacy," Dana said.

"Have you gone through all of Jeff's notes yet?" Mike asked, as Mitch began a search on Shelton, Inc.

"No." He glanced up. "Why?"

Mike hesitated, shrugged. "I don't know. The timing of all this strikes me as odd. How many fires have you investigated in the past three years?"

"Dozens." Mitch didn't get where his brother was going. "What does that have to do with anything?"

"How many fires has Jeff Walker investigated?"

Mitch thought about it for a moment. "Not as many, if you want the truth. Jeff had just turned fifty-two when I took the job and expected me to take a majority of the calls. I took calls two weeks at a time, while he only took one."

"Doesn't sound fair," Dana said with a frown.

"Maybe not, but I also had the most to learn so it made sense to give me more exposure to fire scenes."

"Hmm." Mike's expression was noncommittal.

"Jeff was a nice guy. If I needed help, he was willing to guide me. One thing's for sure, he taught me more than my boss ever did."

Mike looked thoughtful. "Jeff died of a heart attack?"

"Yes." Mitch shook his head. "According to his wife, Tracy, he wasn't feeling well and decided to go lay down instead of going to the ER. He died in his sleep at the age of fifty-five."

"That's terrible." Dana said. "So young."

He nodded. "I know. He wasn't always good about taking care of himself, though. Tracy complained a lot about his refusal to exercise on a regular basis. But still…" He shrugged. "Took everyone by surprise. Our boss, Rick Nelson, was really upset about it."

Mike tapped Jeff's folder. "How long have you had his notes?"

"Less than a week, mostly because Rick's been busy looking for Jeff's replacement. He had a couple of applicants already, but hasn't hired anyone yet. That's why I thought it was strange that Rick wanted to meet with me at the scene of the warehouse fire. I barely had time to review Jeff's notes, much less make any comparisons to the other arson fires we've investigated."

"That's it." Mike lightly smacked his hand on the table. "That's the connection we've been missing."

"What connection? I mean, sure, Rick Nelson left me the message asking to meet him there, but you can't think he's involved in this."

"Maybe, maybe not. But the timing is what's been off. I mean, you've investigated fires for the last three years, but now you're being set up for murder? It has to be linked to Jeff's untimely death."

Mitch stared at his brother in shock. "Are you insinuating that Jeff was somehow covering up arson fires? Deeming them to be accidental by nature instead of set on purpose?"

"Do you have a better explanation?"

No way. Uh-uh. Mitch couldn't believe it. "That doesn't make any sense. Why would he do something like that?"

"Why does anyone?" Mike countered. "Money."

In a flash he remembered the bright yellow convertible Jeff had purchased a few months ago. A ridiculous car to drive in Wisconsin, when winter months clearly outnumbered the summer ones.

And then what about his two kids, a son and a daughter, both attending private colleges on the East Coast? He remembered asking Jeff about that, and his colleague had brushed off his concern, claiming they'd both had been granted generous scholarships.

But what if they hadn't? What if Jeff had gotten a significant influx of money in exchange for declaring the fires accidental?

As much as he hated to admit it, his brother's logic matched the few facts they knew. So far, it was the only motive that made sense for someone setting Mitch up for murder.

TEN

Dana sensed Mitch's distress and wished there was something she could do to help make him feel better. The possible link to Kent's family was bad enough, but adding in Mitch's partner, Jeff, likely being involved in covering up crimes? She couldn't imagine. Mitch must be looking back over the past three years wondering what he had missed.

She rose and moved closer to Mitch, resting her hand on his shoulder. "Let's try to stay focused on the facts. We know Shelton, Inc. owns at least one of the warehouses that burned, but we don't know how many other owners may be involved. And even if Jeff was culpable in covering up the crimes, we still haven't figured out how anyone is making money off the fires in the first place."

Mitch reached up and covered her hand with his, as if grateful for the connection. "Has to be for the insurance money."

"Not necessarily," Mike countered. He stared at their joined hands for a moment, then continued, "What if this is related to construction work of some kind?"

"Simon's muddy work boots," Mitch said thoughtfully.

"Where?"

"In his truck. I noticed them in the back as we fled the apartment complex." Mitch shrugged at the surprise in Mike's eyes. "Hang around with cops long enough and you start to think like them. I was looking for blood or other evidence related to Janice's murder, but there wasn't anything obvious other than the muddy steel-toed construction boots."

"Could be a connection," Mike agreed. "And there was that case a few years back where a well-known construction company was corrupt, with ties to Chicago ."

"So what?" Dana was confused. "I don't understand the link."

Mitch glanced up at her. "Big cities like New York, Chicago and Boston have a history of being associated with the mafia," he explained.

"Mitch is right." Mike's expression was grim. "The wise guys aren't as overt as they used to be, but trust me, the underground world of organized crime still exists."

Despite working in the busy ER of the only level-one trauma center in the city, Dana realized she had led a sheltered life. Caring for victims of crimes was never easy, but she didn't know very much about the true nature of criminal enterprises.

"I'm still not clear why the mafia would want to burn down buildings. What's the payoff for them?" She frowned as realization dawned. "Unless it's about revenge? Or some sort of internal fighting between two criminal organizations?"

"Could be infighting," Mitch agreed. He still hadn't let go of her hand and it was a little scary how much she'd come to appreciate the closeness they shared. "But don't discount the money side. Most business owners carry builder's risk insurance and they can collect on that money if the fire is deemed accidental."

She shivered and moved closer to Mitch, hating the idea of fires being set as a way to profit. "That's terrible."

"Yeah," Mike agreed. "I have an update from Miles."

Mitch's muscles tensed beneath her fingers. "What?"

"ME puts the time of Janice's death somewhere between five and eight in the evening. And you were right, she wasn't killed at the warehouse."

"That's strange, considering it's clear Simon was killed in his apartment," she said. Then realization dawned. "Wait a minute, was she also killed in her own home before being taken to the warehouse?"

"Good thinking," Mike said. "But that's not what happened." He cleared his throat. "Apparently Janice and Simon were living together and as far as we know, there's no evidence that any of her blood was found anywhere inside Simon's apartment."

"You mean, not yet." Mitch tightened his hand over hers then abruptly released it. "I can't believe the entire crime scene has been processed already, considering we found it less than twenty-four hours ago."

"True." Mike's smile didn't reach his eyes. "But for now, let's just say she wasn't there. Do you have any idea where else Janice might have been killed?"

"How would I know?" Mitch jumped to his feet and began to pace the short expanse of the room. "I didn't kill her!"

"I know you didn't but someone set you up as if you did. Which means it must be someplace you would know about. Somewhere you'd be implicated."

"Good thing we already checked out your house," Dana said, striving for a light tone.

"We didn't look in the garage, or the basement," Mitch said.

"Too obvious," Mike countered. "Where else did you meet with her?"

Mitch hunched his shoulders and turned to stare out the window. He was clearly uncomfortable talking about his past relationship with Janice, and Dana couldn't deny the twinge of jealousy.

Stop it, she mentally chided. The poor woman had been brutally murdered. Besides, Mitch had admitted to breaking things off a year ago.

Yet it was clear her being here, listening to the details, bothered him.

"I can—um—leave you guys alone for a bit." She inched toward the connecting door.

Mitch spun from the window. "Don't leave, Dana. This involves both of us now."

He was so close, his woodsy scent clouded her mind, making it difficult to think. "Are you sure? If it's easier to talk about personal stuff without me being here…"

"Stay." His smile was strained, but his clear blue eyes were solemn. "I want you to hear this."

Her heart thudded against her ribs as their gazes clung. Then Mike cleared his throat.

"Maybe *I* should leave," he muttered.

Mitch shot an annoyed glance at his brother. "There are two places we often went, one was down on Barton Beach, at the lakefront, a small picnic spot off the main area. The other was hiking on the trails of Langston Peak, part of the glacier state park. We did some cross-country skiing there, too."

Mike nodded thoughtfully. "Two good possibilities. Which one should we check out first?"

"The lakefront is easier. Not as much surface area to search," Mitch mused.

Dana frowned. "I don't like it. Remember what happened at Simon's apartment? It was almost as if there was someone watching the place, waiting for us to show up so they could send in the police."

"What's our alternative?" Mitch countered. "We don't have much else to go on."

"And we'll be better prepared this time," Mike added. "I can call Noah for backup."

"I hate dragging another officer into this," Mitch protested. "I'd rather Miles and Noah stayed far away, so they don't get in trouble."

"Your call," Mike said with a shrug. "But having them close by just in case the real killer is nearby wouldn't hurt."

Indecision was reflected on Mitch's face, and while she understood his need to protect his family, she hoped and prayed he'd agree to have someone nearby, just in case.

The thought of anything happening to Mitch was unbearable. She depended on him, far more than she should.

It was a no-win situation either way, and Mitch knew it. Risk his brother and brother-in-law or risk Dana.

No contest. His brothers were trained officers. Dana was only involved at all because of him.

He relented with a tiny nod. "Okay, fine. Call Noah. At least he hasn't been formally instructed to arrest me."

Mike looked as if he wanted to argue. "Suit yourself. Give me a few minutes to get in touch with him."

His brother pulled out his phone and walked outside to contact their brother-in-law. Mitch scrubbed his hands over his face, hoping his gut was wrong and that one of the sites where he and Janice used to go wasn't the place she was murdered.

"I still don't know if this is smart," Dana said. "Why not stay here and continue going through Jeff's notes?"

He glanced at the two file folders. "If you were Jeff and had actually changed evidence so that the fires were deemed accidental rather than arson, would you have that kind of detail in your notes?"

She wrinkled her nose. "Probably not."

Mitch still had trouble wrapping his mind around the idea of Jeff being involved. "Some facts he couldn't change, like the ownership of the warehouse, because it had to be reflected in the report."

"Like Shelton, Inc.," Dana said.

"Yes. In order to get money from an insurance policy a formal report has to be turned in. But the rest of the data in here?" He lightly tapped Jeff's file folder. "I have no idea how much is truth and how much is fiction."

"I guess you're right." The doubt in her green eyes belied her words. "I just wish…" Her voice trailed off.

Spending time with Dana made him realize how wrong Janice had been for him. The two women were as different as oceans and mountains and he found himself unbelievably drawn to Dana in a way he hadn't anticipated.

But she was a widow, grieving for a man he hadn't been able to save. And even if she was beginning to come out of her shell, did he want to be the rebound guy?

This situation, being on the run, struggling to find who'd tried to hurt them, wasn't what normal couples went through on a daily basis. Of course forced proximity heightened the senses, creating a false sense of intimacy, making them vulnerable.

Once things returned to normal, who knew if these—feelings shimmering between them would survive?

Besides, he wasn't interested in getting his heart broken again.

"Okay, here's the plan." Mike stepped through the open doorway, tucking his phone in his pocket. "Noah and I are going to drive by Barton Beach to check things out. Give us about fifteen minutes before you head out and keep your disposable phone handy. We'll call you if there's anything amiss."

"The beach is going to be packed on a summer day," he pointed out. "Not sure how you're going to see anything out of place."

"You could be right, but it doesn't hurt to be cautious." Mike pulled out his car keys. "See you later."

"You bet." Mitch glanced at his watch, noting the time. Mike slid behind the wheel of his rental and took off, heading back into town.

"Do you think we should stay another day?" Dana asked.

"Mike thinks we should, but I don't want to waste our money." He didn't add that there was no telling what might happen once they returned to Milwaukee. If he was arrested…

Best not to think the worst.

Dana looked disappointed and he knew being constantly on the move was emotionally draining.

"Let's gather our stuff together," he suggested. "We can always return later this evening."

"Okay." She disappeared between the connecting doors, returning a few minutes later with a small plastic bag of toiletries and the shoe box containing the Glock.

It didn't take the full fifteen minutes to empty the motel room, but Mitch didn't care. Now that he had a destination in mind, he was anxious to get going.

Traffic was light for a Friday. Then again, there were more cars heading out of the city, no doubt with people intending to spend the weekend at the lake. Thirty minutes later, he slowed down as he approached Lakeshore Drive.

"We're supposed to wait for your brother to call," Dana said, breaking the silence.

As if on cue his disposable phone rang. He handed the device to Dana. "Put it on speaker."

She answered the phone. "Mike?"

"Yeah. Where are you guys?"

"Cruising down Lakeshore Drive," Mitch answered. "See anything out of the ordinary?"

"No, although it's crowded, even for a Friday. Where did you and Janice go on the beach?"

"There's a secluded picnic area a hundred yards or so north of the main beach," Mitch said. "There's a path along the shoreline."

"Find a place to park, and we'll meet you there," Mike said.

"Sounds like too many people around," Dana said. "Even if that was the site of the murder, someone would have seen it by now."

"You're right, although it's possible the lake water interfered with the crime scene. Best to check it off the list."

He had to drive around for a bit to find a parking spot. Thanks to the mass of people enjoying the summer day, he and Dana easily blended in.

Mike and Noah were already at the picnic site by the

time he and Dana arrived. "It's clear," Noah said. "No sign of a struggle or any other evidence of a crime."

Mitch knew that meant no blood. He spent a few minutes checking the place out for himself, only to agree with their assessment.

"Langston Peak?" Mike asked.

His gut clenched, but he nodded. "It's the most logical place. But you won't know where to look."

"There must be some kind of landmark," Mike said.

"We used to take one of the lesser known trails, one that led to a large rock." He shrugged. "I can't explain it, but I'll know it when I see it."

Mike and Noah exchanged a glance. "Okay. But this time you really need to let us get up there first. If that's truly the scene of the crime," Noah said. "We'll make sure there isn't anyone lurking around."

"Go, then." He stood for a moment, looking out at Lake Michigan dotted with various boats, some with sails up, gliding with the wind, and others were large speedboats, skipping over the waves.

"You must miss her," Dana said.

"No." He turned to face her. "I miss what I thought we had, but it was nothing more than an illusion." Desperate to change the subject, he spotted the concession stand. "Let's get a soft drink for the road."

Dana nodded and stepped in beside him. But they'd only taken a few steps toward the small building when he noticed the police officer.

"Never mind," he said, sliding his arm around Dana's shoulders and steering her toward the road. "We'll hit a drive-through instead."

Beads of sweat rolled down his temples and not because of the sun overhead. The breeze off the lake was cool enough, but he felt as if the cop's gaze was boring into his back. He pressed a kiss to Dana's forehead as a way to hide his face.

The walk to their parked car seemed to take forever, but they finally made it without being stopped. Mitch didn't waste any time. He opened Dana's door for her and the minute she was situated, he closed her door and then ran behind the SUV to get behind the wheel. It wasn't until he'd gone several miles that he relaxed.

"Maybe we should head back to The Sandpiper," Dana said in a low voice. "Mike and Noah can look for the crime scene."

"They might not be able to find it. There are dozens of trails up there."

There was a sign for a fast-food place up ahead, so he used the drive-through as promised.

"I'll have a lemonade," Dana said.

He ordered two, then eased up to the next window to pay. He decided to use less-traveled highways until he reached the city limits. From there, they made good time on the interstate.

A mile from the entrance to the state park, he gestured to Dana. "Call Mike, let him know we're close."

Dana did as he asked, putting the call on speaker again so they could both hear. "So far it looks good," Mike said. "We're in the parking area and haven't seen anything unusual."

"Good." He was relieved to hear it. "We'll be there in a few minutes."

After paying the nominal fee to get into the state park and putting the tag on his dashboard in view as directed, he spied Mike and Noah's vehicles parked near the back of the lot. There was an obvious empty space between them, so that was where he pulled in.

"Which way?" Mike asked, obviously anxious to get to work.

"To the left." He waited for Dana, then headed off on the trail he and Janice used to hike. At one point, he thought he'd propose to her there, on that rock overlooking the bowl of the glacier, but of course that was before he'd found her with Simon.

He shook off the memories, scanning the area to make sure he was headed the correct way. It had been over a year since he'd been here, and for some strange reason it looked different.

After five minutes down one trail, he stopped abruptly. "Sorry, this isn't it."

Once again, Mike and Noah exchanged a questioning glance.

"Give me a break, it's been a while." He retraced his steps and took another path.

Ten yards in, he wondered if he was losing his mind, when a glimpse of a small brown circle at the edge of a green leaf caught his eye.

He stopped so abruptly, Mike bumped into him from behind.

"Are you lost again?"

"No. Look at this." Mitch dropped to one knee to get a better look and Mike joined him. "We should have brought evidence bags."

"I have a few." Noah pulled one from the back pocket of his jeans. "What is it?"

"I'm not sure." Mitch gingerly picked up the stained leaf and dropped it into the evidence bag. "Let's keep going."

Two steps later, there was another dark round circle. Then another.

"Is that blood?" Dana asked in a hoarse whisper.

He was very much afraid it was. Quickening his pace, he kept going along the trail until he reached a part where the bloodstains made a small puddle.

"This is definitely blood," Mike said in a grim tone. "We'll need to take samples to be sure, but I'm betting that whoever killed Janice came this way."

Mitch's chest was so tight he couldn't speak. The rock overlooking the glacier basin was mostly hidden by the thick brush. He eased the branches out of the way to get a better look.

The rock was covered in old, dried blood.

He turned back and looked again at the small puddle of blood safely away from his brother's feet and the subsequent drops of blood leading away from the area.

It was easy enough to imagine the killer had used a fireman's carry to get Janice's body out of there. Most firefighters kept themselves physically fit.

Yet another reason for the police to believe he was the primary suspect.

ELEVEN

Seeing the rock surface stained with blood and Mitch's pale expression, Dana stepped forward to place a reassuring hand on his arm. He must have been completely lost in his thoughts, as he didn't react in any way.

"Listen, Mitch, we need to call this in." Noah pulled his phone out of his pocket. "You and Dana should hit the road, so that you're far away before the authorities arrive."

"No, I disagree." Mike put out his hand to cover the phone, so his brother-in-law couldn't use it. "The cops will suspect right away that Mitch pointed us to this area, because who else would know that this was a spot he and Janice came to on a regular basis? Better if we left an anonymous tip, from a phone that can't be traced."

"I'll do it." Mitch's voice was flat and dull. "We can use Dana's disposable phone."

Dana frowned. "I don't get it. Why do we have to make the call at all? We came out here to prove Mitch was being framed by someone who knew these types of personal details about him. So now we feel certain that this is the scene of Janice's murder. But shouldn't we be looking for clues pointing toward the real murderer?"

"She's right," Noah agreed. "But without forensics, there's no way to know if the real murderer left any blood and/or trace evidence behind. Which is why we need to call it in, before the scene degrades any further. What if it rains?"

"Wait. How was she transported?" Mitch abruptly asked. "I used my personal truck to go to the warehouse that night. There for sure wasn't any blood inside, other than maybe my own from my neck wound."

Mike nodded thoughtfully. "Where is your personal truck now?"

"Probably still in the hospital parking structure, right?" Dana said, looking at Mitch, who nodded in agreement.

"Unless it's been towed," Mike muttered.

She shrugged. "It might eventually get towed, but I doubt that's happened yet. Trust me, patients drive themselves to the ER all the time and then end up admitted to the hospital. I've heard of cars staying for weeks."

"Still, we should get it out of there ASAP," Mike said.

She couldn't disagree.

"Which brings up another point. Mitch, don't you have access to a work vehicle?" Noah asked.

Mitch's expression turned grim. "Yeah, I do. I used it earlier in the day on Wednesday, same day I was directed to meet Rick at the warehouse. Only I left it parked in the lot of the Public Safety Administration building, downtown."

There was a tense moment of silence as the implication sunk in. "I don't like to admit it, but I'm thinking that it was used to move Janice's body from here to the warehouse where she was found," Mike said.

"Let's go." Mitch's expression turned hard as stone. "If someone else used the vehicle, there's a good chance that trace evidence from the killer was also left behind."

"*We* aren't going anywhere," Noah said, putting up his hand. "You and Dana are going to return to the motel. Leave the rest of this to me and Mike."

"No way. We only have two vehicles but I know where I left the one I used. Could be the killer wasn't smart enough to return it in the exact same spot. Like it or not, I'm coming with you."

Dana wanted to protest. In her opinion, Mitch should stay far away from the admin building. What if it was a trap? Yet she wasn't about to be left behind, either. If he went, she was going, too. She bit her lip and waited to see if Mike and Noah would continue to press their argument.

The two men exchanged a resigned look. "Okay. If you want to come, that's fine, but we need to figure out a way to keep you out of sight."

"Wouldn't it be better to wait until nighttime?" Dana asked. "Less people around."

"I don't think so," Mitch countered. "In my opinion, we'd have a better chance of blending in during business hours."

"Popping the trunk to see if there's blood inside might attract some attention," Mike drawled. "But I agree, the more cars in the lot and on the street, the easier to blend in."

"Okay, let's go." Mitch took her hand. "We'll meet you downtown. We'll also call in an anonymous tip related to this crime scene here, on the way."

"Hold off on that," Mike suggested. "I know you're worried about losing trace evidence, but maybe we can point them toward the vehicle instead. There's a higher likelihood of finding something in a car that's been protected from the elements compared to anything that may have been left out here."

Noah grimaced, obviously not thrilled with the idea of not calling in a crime scene.

Mitch looked at Dana, as if interested in her opinion. She shrugged. "I agree with Mike on this one. If blood is found in the car, then any tip that's called in should include both areas. It's the best chance of finding the identity of the real killer."

Mitch nodded. "Okay, then we'll wait." He glanced back toward the rock hidden behind the trees. "It's not as if another couple of hours will make a difference."

Noah didn't say anything, but she sensed he'd go along with Mitch's plan.

She and Mitch fell into step behind Noah and Mike on the path that would lead them back to the parking lot.

"Are you okay?" she asked, breaking the prolonged silence.

He shook his head. "I hate knowing that two people died over money and greed. It's not right."

"Of course it's not right." She tightened her fingers around his. "Desperate people do desperate things. I see it all the time in the emergency department." She thought for a minute about Kent's family and their wealth. How would they cope if they suddenly lost everything? She suspected they wouldn't handle it well at all. "In my opinion, money can be as addictive as a drug. Often people aren't satisfied with what they have. They constantly want more. To the point that nothing else matters, not even someone's life."

"That's a really interesting analogy," Mitch said. He looked thoughtful for a moment, then quoted, "'Better the little that the righteous have than the wealth of many wicked.'"

"Is that from the Bible?" she guessed.

"*Psalm* 37:16. Seemed appropriate."

She hadn't read the Bible outside of what was preached in church, but she'd always enjoyed quotes from the *Book of Psalms*. "I like it, too."

"Stop," Mike hissed in a low voice.

She and Mitch froze. "What?" Mitch whispered.

"There's a Department of Natural Resources vehicle parked right beside my car," Noah said. "Could be a co-incidence, but you and Dana need to stay back while we check things out."

Mitch immediately took several steps backward, moving deeper into the surrounding foliage. She stayed close at his side, gripping his hand nervously.

Her fears of this being a possible trap for Mitch didn't seem too far off the mark. The best-case scenario was that Mitch would be arrested for a double homicide.

The worst case? That she and Mitch would both be silenced, permanently.

Mitch drew Dana off the trail, into the woods. "Walk as quietly as possible," he whispered near her ear.

She nodded, clutching his hand as if it was a lifeline.

He was fortunate to know this entire area so well—or maybe it was too well, since Janice had been murdered here. The woods grew dense to the west, so that was the direction he took.

Scanning the area, he searched his memory. He knew there was a grove of thick pine trees that might offer some protection.

There!

He adjusted their trajectory, stepping carefully over rocks and branches while avoiding the thorn bushes. Once he reached the pine trees, he drew Dana close to his side so he could whisper, "This is a decent hiding spot, so stay here. I'll be back shortly."

"Where are you going?"

He knew she wasn't going to like it. "I want to see who is in the parking lot, see if it's anyone I recognize."

"I'll come with you."

"I need to know you're safe. And I won't be long." He didn't add that it would be faster and easier for him to move through the woods without her. "I just need a few minutes."

Dana reluctantly nodded. "All right, but please hurry."

"If I'm not back in fifteen minutes, call Mike." He punched his brother's number into his disposable phone, then handed it to her.

She took the phone with a strained smile. "Be careful."

"Always." He stared down at her for a moment, fighting the urge to pull her close and kiss her senseless. Somehow he found the strength to turn away. Moving between the trees, he used the map in his head to guide him to a spot that would provide a view of the parking lot.

Five minutes later, he knelt next to the trunk of a large black walnut tree. His heart sank when he noticed the DNR officer dressed in the traditional uniform of a brown shirt and dark green slacks talking to Mike and Noah. The Department of Natural Resources had jurisdiction over state parkland, and he was pretty sure that included homicide investigations.

Getting law enforcement agencies to work together was always a challenge. Sure, logically it made sense that they should, but he knew that egos and hierarchies typically got in the way.

It occurred to Mitch that the killer had made a mistake, choosing this site to murder Janice. In the murderer's effort to frame Mitch, he'd either forgotten or hadn't realized the different jurisdictions involved. Actually, three so far…the Milwaukee PD for the warehouse, the Oakdale Police for Simon's murder and now the DNR.

As a fire investigator, he crossed jurisdictions all the time. It was too expensive for each police municipality to have their own investigators, so between him and Jeff, they'd covered all of the districts in the greater Milwaukee area.

Jeff's death had left him as the only investigator. Now that he was on the run and in hiding, the role would fall to his boss, Rick Nelson.

Had that been the plan all along? Mitch didn't want to believe his boss was involved in this. But looking back over the past twenty-four to forty-eight hours, Rick seemed the most likely suspect. The initial call had come from Rick's office. Rick had access to his work vehicle and knew about Mitch's breakup with Janice. It wouldn't be hard to figure out that Janice and Simon were dating.

But how did Jeff fit in? Were both Jeff and Rick involved in a payoff to declare fires as accidental? Had Jeff's heart attack and unexpected death put a wrench in their scheme? If so, why hadn't Rick just kept all of Jeff's files, rather than handing them over to Mitch? Yes, it would have looked odd to Mitch for his boss to keep them, but it wouldn't have been his place to argue, either.

He glanced at his watch, wincing when he realized he'd already used half his allotted time. Then he noticed the DNR officer was walking away from Mike and Noah. Mitch hesitated, wondering if the guy was calling for reinforcements, but the officer slid behind the wheel and drove away.

Relief washed over him. He stood and quickly made his way back to where Dana waited.

"You sound like an elephant thundering through here," she whispered as he approached.

"I know, but the danger is over, at least for now. I'm not sure what Mike and Noah said to the DNR officer, but he left."

"Good, because the mosquitos are eating me alive." She slapped at one that landed on her arm.

He led the way through the woods back to the trail. From there, it was a short hike to meet up with Noah and Mike.

"What did he want?" Mitch asked.

Noah grimaced. "I was stupid and forgot to put the tag on my windshield."

"Good thing you had it handy," Mike said. "I was worried he'd ask for our names and occupations. That might have led to questions we wouldn't have wanted to answer."

"Would the DNR know about the BOLO issued for Mitch?" Dana asked. "I would think not."

"Maybe, maybe not, but it was still a risk I wasn't willing to take," Mike said. "Let's get out of here."

Mitch was anxious to leave, too. He really wanted to get downtown to the Public Safety Administration office building.

"I'd like a blood sample first." Noah opened the back door to his car and pulled out an evidence bag and a sterile cotton swab. "Shouldn't take long."

Noah jogged up the trail, disappearing from view. Mitch glanced at his brother. "We'll meet up with you downtown."

Mike didn't look happy, but nodded. "Yeah, okay. But don't touch anything until we get there, understand?

And you need to make sure there isn't anyone hanging around, watching the place, waiting for you to show up."

"I understand." He urged Dana toward Hawk's SUV. "See you soon."

The trip back to Milwaukee didn't take long, although he had to stop for gas. The hour was well past lunchtime, but he wasn't very hungry. Seeing the area where Janice had been brutally murdered had made him lose his appetite.

He took the 13th Street exit, then made his way toward the Public Safety Administration building. "Keep your eyes on the parking lot," he advised. "The vehicles we use are white and are labeled Fire Investigation along the side."

Dana stared intently out her window, which was good because he had to keep his eyes on the road.

"Notice anything unusual?" he asked after the first pass.

"No, and I couldn't see any white cars with lettering along the sides, either."

He turned left to go around the block. "I'm going to go past it again. This time look at the northeast corner of the lot. That's where I left it."

A few minutes later, he once again drove past the parking lot. He did his best to pick out the vehicle, but without success.

"It's not there," Dana said. "Is that good news or bad?"

"I have no clue." He didn't like it. There should be two cars, unless Rick Nelson was driving one. The other should have been where he left it.

"Pull over," Dana said.

"Why?"

"It will be easier for me to walk through the lot rather than to keep driving past."

"I'd rather not." But the light turned red and when he stopped, Dana used that moment to slide out of the car.

"Wait," he said, but she slammed the door shut and darted around the vehicle to the sidewalk. "Stubborn woman," he muttered.

The light turned green, so he made another loop around the block. It seemed to take forever, partially because he hit every single red light, and when he made it to the front of the building again, he saw Dana waiting for him. He pulled over so she could get in, ignoring the irritated honking from the driver behind him.

"Not there," Dana said as she clipped her seat belt together. "There was only one white car and it was a Mazda, no letters stenciled on the side."

Mitch tightened his grip on the steering wheel. "Where on earth could it be?" Then, suddenly, he knew. "My garage."

Dana's eyes widened. "Of course. That makes perfect sense. First they put the vehicle in your garage, then they hid the gun in your closet."

He sighed. "It's ridiculously obvious. Only an idiot would set himself up like that."

"Maybe, but it's also just a theory. Considering there are cops watching your place, we won't be able to prove it."

"Not right now, but we can always sneak in again later tonight." He glanced at her. "We were successful the first time."

"Are you serious? Don't you remember how we were almost caught?"

"But we weren't. Do you still have my phone?" She nodded. "Call Mike. Let him know the administrative building is a bust and that we're going back to the motel."

She pulled out the phone. "Maybe we should check Simon's apartment complex."

"That's brilliant." And something he should have thought of, as well. "Tell Mike to meet us there."

Dana made the call, using the speaker option so he could listen in. "We're heading to Oakdale," she said. "Neither one of the fire investigation vehicles is at the administrative building, so we're checking the parking lot behind Simon's apartment building. Mitch wants you to meet us there."

"Will do. But stay out of sight until we know the coast is clear."

She disconnected the call, glancing over at him. "Do you really think the vehicle will be there?"

"I don't know, but it's worth checking out. If it's not there, then all the more reason to check out my place later tonight."

"I don't want you to go," Dana murmured. "It's too dangerous. Even if the car is there, what does that mean for us? Are you really going to call in an anonymous tip about Langston Peak and the vehicle parked in your garage? Why not just hand over the gun in the shoe box, too?"

He didn't have a good response to that, so he remained silent.

They reached the Oakdale city limits fifteen minutes later, and instead of driving past Simon's apartment complex, he pulled into the Gas 'N Go station. "Why don't you stay here?"

She narrowed her gaze. "Yeah, right. That's not an option. Are we going in through the field?"

He nodded. "Yes. Figured we can check out the cars

easier on foot since all the parking lots are tucked behind the buildings."

She held out his phone. "Are you going to call your brother?"

"Not yet, but hang on to it." He pushed out of the car and headed toward the back of the building. They'd be out in the open while crossing the field, so he hesitated for a moment.

He swept his glance over the area. Nothing looked out of place. He wasn't a cop like his brothers, but he still trusted his instincts. It was broad daylight late on a Friday afternoon, and he figured the worst-case scenario was that there might be a cop making rounds, watching the area.

"Ready?" Dana asked.

"Yes. We're going to head for that blue truck parked at the end of the closest parking lot."

"I see it."

"Let's go." Mitch took the lead, crossing the field in a direct line toward the blue Chevy. They'd almost made it to the truck when he caught the glimpse of movement from the corner of his eye.

He looked to his right in time to see a man rise to his feet holding a strange-looking weapon.

A tranquilizer gun!

"Get down," he shouted to Dana as he leaped in front of her. He heard a pop then felt something sharp pierce his shoulder.

He yanked out the dart as quickly as he could, but the drug must have gotten into his system, because he began to feel woozy. He fought off the wave of dizziness, continuing to move toward the parking lot and the shelter offered there.

Dana was talking on the phone while pushing at him

from behind. Three yards, then two, then one. He did his best to keep her covered with his body, expecting a second dart to hit him at any moment.

The truck wavered in his line of vision. He reached the side, leaning heavily against it. "Stay out of sight until Mike can get here."

"He's close. We just have to hang on for a few more minutes."

He tried to nod, then felt himself falling to his knees. What had been laced on the tip of the dart anyway?

"Hang on, Mitch. Do you hear me? Stay awake."

But he couldn't. His last conscious thought was that his bad decision made him fail in his promise to keep Dana safe.

TWELVE

"Come on, Mitch." Dana crouched over Mitch's heavy frame, where he was slumped against the side of the truck. She shook him, hoping he'd wake up. "You're too heavy for me to lift. I need you to help me."

But Mitch didn't answer.

Her chest squeezed with alarm. He was out cold and she'd never felt so helpless. What kind of drug had been absorbed into Mitch's bloodstream? What if it was poison? No, it had to be a sedative, right? Why would they risk poison showing up on a toxicology screen?

She hovered over Mitch's slumped figure, keeping an eye on the reassuring rise and fall of his chest. She glanced at some movement off to her right, shocked to see Mike driving across the field like it was an all-terrain vehicle rather than a car. The way it bounced up and over the ruts and weeds made her fear he'd roll over.

Hurry, she thought. Then she sent up a quick prayer. *Please, Lord, give Mike and Noah the strength they need to rescue us.*

She placed a hand on Mitch's chest to monitor his breathing while watching Mike approach. It was hard to tell where the guy with the dart gun was located, and she worried he might have a real gun, too.

Should she call 911? Or wait until they could get Mitch into Mike's SUV? Her decision was made for her when Mike was close enough for her to see the concerned determination in his gaze.

Slipping her arm beneath Mitch's armpit, she used all her strength in an attempt to get him off the ground. She didn't get very far.

Noah lowered the passenger-side window. "Stay down. We'll help get him into the car."

She nodded in relief and bent her head to rest her cheek on Mitch's head. "Don't worry, we're going to get you to the hospital ASAP."

Mitch didn't move or acknowledge her in any way. Was his breathing getting slower? She pressed her fingertips against his carotid artery, relaxing a bit when she found his pulse.

Mike's SUV stopped just a couple feet away. Noah shot out of the passenger door and dropped to his knees on Mitch's other side. "Okay, we need to get him into the back seat as quickly as possible."

"I know." She took a deep breath, once again asking God to send her strength. "Let's do it."

With Noah supporting Mitch on the other side, she levered upright, staggering beneath his dead weight. Somehow, they half-dragged, half-carried Mitch to the SUV. Getting him inside wasn't as simple as it sounded, but they managed. After what seemed like forever, Mitch was lying on his side, his upper torso and head along the seat, his legs awkwardly bent so that his feet were jammed on the floor.

Dana crawled in after him, kneeling on the floor behind Mike's driver's seat. There wasn't much room, but at least she could monitor Mitch's pulse and breathing from there.

"Go," Noah shouted, slamming the door behind her. He leaped into the passenger seat as Mike hit the gas.

"We need to take him straight to Trinity Medical Center," Dana said as they bumped up and into the parking lot onto pavement. "I have no idea what they drugged him with."

"That might be the first place they look for us," Mike pointed out. "I know you work there, but maybe a different hospital would be a better choice."

"I know the doctors at Trinity," she protested. "And they're well equipped to run various toxicology panels. I don't know if I trust a smaller hospital to have the same resources."

There was a long silence and she wished she could see their faces.

"Listen, we can drive in through the ambulance bay." It wasn't meant for general public access, but too bad, she didn't care if she got in trouble for not following the rules. "That way the car will be out of view. And if the ER isn't too busy and I can call in a few favors, I'm sure we can get Mitch an antidote and be out before they find us."

"That's a lot of ifs," Mike said. "But okay, we'll do it."

"What about searching for Mitch's work car?" Noah asked. "Maybe you should let me out so I can head back to find it."

Mike snorted. "Yeah, right. As if I want to face Maddy's wrath doing something like that. Did you get a good look at the guy with the dart gun?"

"No," Noah admitted.

"I didn't, either," Dana offered. "I saw Mitch flinch when the dart hit him, and he reacted quickly by yanking it out, but I wish I still had it. It would be easier to know how to treat him."

"It's probably a sedative of some sort," Mike said.

Dana hoped he was right, but couldn't get the idea of a possible poison out of her mind.

The drive to Trinity was quick, although it seemed endless. But when they were close, she told Mike how to find the ambulance bay. When he pulled in, no one came out to meet them, because they hadn't called the paramedic base ahead of time.

Dana pushed out of the car and ran inside to get assistance. Thankfully one of her favorite ER docs, Dr. Ramsey, was nearby. "My friend was shot by a dart gun with an unknown substance. He's unconscious. I need a gurney."

"You came in through the ambulance bay?" Dr. Ramsey asked in surprise.

"Yes." She wasn't about to apologize for it, either. "Please hurry."

There was a gurney off to the side of the hallway, so she pushed it into the ambo bay. Mike and Noah were already working on getting Mitch out of the back seat, literally holding him upright.

Within minutes, they were able to get Mitch on the gurney. Dr. Ramsey and one of Dana's colleagues, Noelle Curtis, wheeled him back inside.

"Take him to trauma bay two and register him as a Male Doe," Dr. Ramsey directed. Then he looked at Dana. "What happened to his neck?"

"He was attacked a few days ago. Dr. Crowley stitched him up, then I had to replace a few sutures because they broke open. He may need a dose of antibiotics."

Dr. Ramsey sighed. "Okay, fine. You need to stay back, out of our way. You're not on duty here, understand?"

"Of course." Twisting her fingers together, she moved backward to the corner of the trauma bay, watching as the team began assessing and working on Mitch. Noelle hooked him up to a heart monitor and the steady beep of his heart helped keep her calm. Another nurse, Amy, drew several tubes of blood for the tox screen. All the while, Dr. Ramsey stood at the foot of the gurney, directing care. Once the nurses had completed a set of vital signs, he stepped forward and peered at Mitch's eyes, shook his head at the sutures in his neck, then tried to shake him awake.

"Pupils are dilated, possible narcotics on board," Dr. Ramsey said as he slipped his penlight back into his breast pocket. He returned to the foot of the gurney. "Get an IV started, and give him 0.2 milligrams of Narcan. Hopefully that will bring him around."

Dana couldn't tear her gaze away. Noelle expertly placed an IV and then administered the medication.

No response.

Dana's stomach clenched with fear, and she felt Mike and Noah coming up to stand on either side of her. But she couldn't look away, or speak. Her entire being was focused on the man lying inert on the hospital gurney.

"Give a 500 cc fluid bolus," Dr. Ramsey said. "Then let's try another 0.2 of Narcan."

Still no response.

"One more time," Dr. Ramsey directed. "Another fluid bolus followed by a third dose of Narcan. If that doesn't work, we'll go to 0.2 of flumazenil."

Dana held her breath, watching and waiting for a reaction. She hoped the Narcan worked, because flumazenil could cause seizures, among other side effects.

But the third dose of Narcan was the charm. Mitch's legs jerked reflexively and she let her pent-up breath out in a sigh of relief.

"He's going to be fine," she said, finally glancing over at Mike. "He's starting to come around."

"What kind of narcotic did they use in that dart gun?" Mike asked. "I've heard there are drugs strong enough to drop an elephant."

"That's true." She swallowed hard. "We won't know for sure until Mitch's blood tests come back and the results are matched up with whatever is in the dart Mitch has is tested. But the fact that it was difficult to bring Mitch around makes me suspect they used a new narcotic called carfentanil. It's an incredibly dangerous medication, ten thousand times more potent than morphine. With the heroin crisis in the city, it appears people are looking for something stronger. We're starting to see overdoses related to the street use of carfentanil, and many of them have died."

"Street use, huh?" Mike's gaze narrowed. "If that's what he's using in those darts, we need to get the guy with the tranq gun off the street, permanently."

She silently agreed, but for right now, all she cared about was that Mitch was okay. Pulling out the dart must have helped dilute the medication, because anyone taking carfentanil for the first time had a high likelihood of dying from respiratory failure.

Had that been the goal? To take Mitch out? What about the theory that the dart gun was to take them out long enough to stage a murder-suicide?

She didn't know what to think anymore. Her chest tightened and she felt dizzy as she realized just how close she'd come to losing Mitch.

Forever.

* * *

The bright lights overhead made him wince in agony. Where was he? What had happened to him?

And most important, where was Dana?

He struggled to lift his right arm, but it felt as if it weighed a hundred pounds. His movements were clumsy, and in his attempt to shield his eyes from the glare, he smacked himself in the head.

"Don't do that."

The strange female voice wasn't at all reassuring. He sensed there were several people around him. Had he been captured by the guy with the dart gun? Was Dana captured, too?

Lord, help me! Keep Dana safe!

A sense of calm washed over him and he held himself still, gathering his strength and waiting for a chance to make his move. He flexed his wrists, noting he wasn't tied down, so that was good. Voices surrounded him, but he couldn't understand exactly what they were saying, so he blocked them out, concentrating instead on taking slow, deep breaths.

He wasn't going to just lie here while Dana might be in trouble. Hands moved over him. Maybe the guys were searching for a hidden weapon?

He wished he'd purchased ammunition for the Glock.

The touching stopped and he took one last deep breath and levered himself upright. Beeping alarms went crazy and hands grabbed at him, but he desperately fought them off, determined to get away.

"Mitch, what are you doing? Stop it, you're going to hurt yourself! Mitch, please! Stop!"

Dana? He pried his eyes open. Now that the light wasn't directly above him, it was easier to see. His vision was blurry, but Dana's frightened expression shot straight to his heart.

"Are you okay?" He blinked, struggled to focus. "You're not hurt?"

"No, but you are. Please stop fighting us. You're in the hospital." Her small hands pressed gently yet firmly against his chest. "The doctor is trying to flush the drugs out of your system."

The hospital? Suddenly it all made sense. The people, the lights, the beeping.

They hadn't been captured by the bad guys.

He remembered going to Simon's apartment complex and being hit with the dart gun. How long had he been out of it?

He remained sitting upright on the edge of the cot or bed or whatever he was on. Lying down felt too vulnerable. Not to mention the overhead lights shining in his eyes gave him a headache.

"Hey, bro, you're scaring the staff." Mike's deep voice was reassuring. "The sooner you rest up, the sooner we're out of here."

He knew Mike was right. The bad guys could easily find them there—after all, they had before. "Water," he said in a hoarse voice. His mouth and throat felt as if he'd swallowed a bottle of sand.

"Here." Dana held a cup with a straw to his lips. He felt ridiculous, but drank anyway.

"I think we can safely move him to a bed in the arena," a deep voice said. "He'll be fine."

"Thanks, but we really need to get out of here," Mitch said. His vision began to clear, which was good. Now if he could get his strength and coordination back, they'd be even better.

"Not until you get a dose of antibiotics." The male

voice belonged to a man in his late thirties, wearing green scrubs. He had a name tag on that read Dr. Ramsey, MD. "The sutures in your neck look red and inflamed. Could be infected."

Mitch wanted to argue, but the stubbornness in Dana's gaze made him sigh. How long could it take to get a dose of antibiotics? "Okay, but make it quick."

"Any allergies I need to know about?" the doc asked.

"Not that I know of."

"Good." The doctor rattled off the name of some medication he'd never heard of, and one of the nurses went over to what looked like a giant ATM machine to get what she needed. Within minutes, the antibiotic was dripping in through his IV.

"How long have I been here?" he asked, looking at Dana then his brother.

"Almost ninety minutes," Mike answered. "Don't worry, we'll be on the road shortly."

Not soon enough, but he didn't say anything more. Ignoring the sense of urgency wasn't easy. He kept glancing at the tiny bag hooked to his IV, wondering if they'd slowed it down on purpose to keep him here longer.

He felt okay, not 100 percent, but good enough to move under his own power. To prove it, he slid off the edge of the gurney, standing up on his own two feet.

"Easy," Dana said, putting a hand on his arm. "You might still have some of that narcotic in your system."

"Narcotic?" He scowled, not liking the sound of that.

"I'll fill you in on the details later," Mike said. "How much longer?" His brother looked at Dana.

"Ten minutes, maybe less."

"Okay. Noah and I will get the car and bring it back to the ambulance bay. We'll meet you there shortly."

Mitch was all in favor of that plan. He gestured to the IV. "Can't you speed this thing up a bit?"

"No." Dana glared at him. "Be glad I'm not making you stay longer for observation."

"We have his lab results back," Dr. Ramsey said. "His white count is up a bit, so you'll need antibiotics for the road. Also the tox screen confirms he was injected with carfentanil." Ramsey's expression was grim. "A highly powerful narcotic that we've been seeing on the streets lately. You're lucky to be alive."

Dana made a soft sound of distress and moved closer to him. He hugged her close, knowing that the fault rested squarely on his shoulders.

He should have waited for Mike and Noah to arrive. Or better yet, let his brother do the investigating for him. There was no really good reason for him to insist on seeing the crime scene for himself.

However, he was the one being framed, a personal attack of the worst kind. One he still didn't understand.

"The rest of his labs are fairly normal," Dr. Ramsey continued. "My advice is to rest, continue with antibiotics and drink lots of fluids."

"Would you be willing to give us a few days' worth of antibiotics to hold us over until we can fill a prescription?" Dana asked, her voice tentative. "I know I'm asking for a lot of favors here, but it's important we get out of here as soon as possible."

"Dana, are you in trouble?" Dr. Ramsey asked with a frown. "I think it's best if we call the police."

"No!" Mitch's knee-jerk response came out sharper than he intended. At the dark suspicion in Ramsey's eyes, he hastily backtracked. "What I meant to say was that my brother-in-law, Noah Sinclair, is a MPD cop. And my other brother Miles is a homicide detective."

That was true, even if Miles wasn't actually involved in the situation. "We have the help of the authorities already."

"Dana, may I speak to you in private?" Dr. Ramsey obviously wasn't convinced.

He was surprised when Dana didn't move. "He's right," she said. "Noah is a cop and so are two of Mitch's brothers. We're fine, really. If you can't provide the extra doses of antibiotics, I understand, just give us the prescription."

Dr. Ramsey stood there as if weighing his options when his pager began to shrill. He unclipped it from his belt, read the message on the small screen and grimaced. "Trauma alert, GSW to the head." He replaced the pager and gestured to one of the nurses. "Go ahead and give them enough oral antibiotics to hold them over for a few days. Then get set up for the incoming gunshot wound."

Mitch let out his breath in a relieved sigh along with a tiny splash of guilt. The doc was right that Dana should go to the police for protection. Something to think about. He glanced up at the mini IV bag; it was nearly empty.

"Thanks, Noelle," Dana said, accepting a small white bag a nurse handed to her. "I appreciate everything you've done."

"Hope everything will be all right," the nurse said, throwing a suspicious look at Mitch. "If you need help, give me a call."

"I will, thanks." Dana's smile was strained and Mitch felt lower and slimier than a worm. "Will you disconnect his antibiotic now and remove the IV?"

Noelle nodded and went to work. Two minutes later, he was free to go. Dana wrapped her arm around his waist, as if she was afraid he'd keel over. She led the way down the corridor and then to the right, where there was a spacious area, wide enough for three ambulances to be parked side by side.

The only vehicle in there was Mike's rented SUV. He slid into the back seat next to Dana.

Mike pulled away, glancing at Mitch over his shoulder. "You sure you're feeling okay?"

"I'm fine." Or he would be. He felt sick to his stomach, probably from all the meds he'd been given. "Where are we headed?"

Mike and Noah looked at each other. "Back to The Sandpiper Motel for now," Noah said. "You're clearly in danger, Mitch. It's best if you stay out of sight from here on."

"You've got it wrong," Mitch argued. "That dart wasn't intended for me."

"What do you mean?" Mike asked sharply.

He reached over and took Dana's hand in his. "I jumped in front of Dana. Both attempts with the dart gun were aimed at her. She's the one in danger, maybe even more so than me."

A heavy silence filled the interior of the car. Mitch knew that it was true, but he still didn't understand the motive.

Were they trying to silence Dana simply because she'd helped him? Or because they were worried she knew something about what was really going on, details about the Shelton family business?

Either way, this latest attempt solidified the truth. One way or another, Kent's family was definitely involved.

THIRTEEN

A chill rippled down Dana's spine as Mitch's words echoed over and over in her mind.

Was it possible she'd been the target? She tried to think back to their dash across the field. Everything had happened so fast, but now that she replayed those few seconds, she realized Mitch was right.

He had jumped in front of her, the dart hitting him high in the shoulder. The dose of carfentanil had been strong enough to knock Mitch out, might even have been strong enough to kill him.

It certainly would have done worse to someone lighter and smaller.

Like her.

But why? Because she'd helped Mitch escape the hospital that night? It seemed crazy that someone would try to kill her for that. Why not just aim to hit Mitch in the first place?

"Are you sure there's nothing you remember about Kent's family?" Mitch asked.

She shrugged helplessly. "I've told you what I know. Kent's mother's maiden name is Shelton and Kent's family works in real estate. I have no idea why anyone would want to hurt me because of that information. It's public record."

"True." Mitch's expression was grim.

"Okay, here's the plan," Mike said, interrupting them. "We're going to drop you both off at the motel, then we'll head back to see if we can find the vehicle you use for official business."

"We need a car," Mitch protested. "Otherwise we're sitting ducks if someone finds us."

Noah grimaced, then nodded. "He's right. Let's go back and pick up my ride."

"If we're going back, we may as well pick up Hawk's car," Mitch argued. "Better to keep far away from anything linked to the Callahan name."

"Isn't Hawk's car compromised already?" Dana glanced between the men. "Wouldn't tranq gun guy have spotted it?"

"I muddied up the license plate," Mitch pointed out. "One black SUV looks much like another."

"I'll use Hawk's SUV," Mike said. "You can use this rental. I didn't use my own name, so it should be safe enough for a while."

The offer helped Dana feel better. Who knew how difficult it would be to go on the run from people who had access to personal information? If it wasn't for Mitch's family, they'd have been caught a long time ago.

The near miss outside Simon's apartment building made her shiver. The way Mitch had put his life on the line in order to protect her was humbling. How could anyone believe a man as honorable as Mitch would kill Janice and Simon?

Even as the thought entered her head, she understood that a man's reputation and character wouldn't mean squat when compared to the overwhelming physical evidence stacked against him.

"The gun!" She glanced at Mitch in horror. "We left it in Hawk's SUV."

"What gun?" Noah and Mike asked simultaneously.

She winced, remembering that Mitch hadn't mentioned finding the weapon in his closet at home.

"The murder weapon," Mitch said in a resigned tone. "We found it in my closet the night I sneaked into my place to get my notes."

"It was put in a shoe box with the cover lifted up in one corner," Dana added. "We didn't want to leave it behind in case we didn't get back to the motel."

"Great," Mike muttered. "That's just great. Any other evidence we need to know about?"

"No." Mitch sounded exhausted, as if beaten down by the events of the day. "They have my fingerprints and blood at the warehouse, the scene of Janice's murder was at a place where we used to hang out and the murder weapon was found in the closet of my bedroom."

"Hopefully it's still in the SUV," Noah said. "If not…"

There was nothing but silence as Mike drove back toward the Gas 'N Go station. Mike didn't go straight to their vehicles, but swung past, checking the area for cops or other police authorities.

The area was oddly quiet, as if nothing had transpired a few hours earlier. No cops, no people hanging around in clusters, talking.

Nothing.

She didn't like it. Granted, the tranq gun wasn't loud like a regular rifle, but surely someone had seen Mitch go down and Mike driving like a maniac across the field to pick them up.

"Something's wrong," she said. "It's as if nothing happened here."

"Yeah," Noah agreed. "It's eerie."

"Could be that the cops came, didn't find anything and left," Mitch pointed out.

"Maybe." Mike didn't sound convinced. "Mitch, give Noah your keys. I'll let him out here so he can double back on foot to get Hawk's SUV."

Mitch dug in his pocket, then handed over the keys to Noah. "Thanks, man. I know you're putting your career on the line for me."

"Hey, I'm part of the Callahan family now, and we stick together no matter what."

Dana felt a strange sense of envy for the closeness the Callahans shared. Even with Noah, who wasn't a brother by blood, but was accepted as such anyway.

"The shoe box is tucked beneath the passenger seat," she said. "If it's still there at all."

"Okay, I'll check." The moment Mike pulled over to the curb, Noah pushed open his passenger door and hopped out. "See you at The Sandpiper."

"Be safe," Mike said. "Maddy will be upset with me if something happens to you."

Noah flashed a cheeky grin and then shut the door. Mike didn't stick around, but eased into traffic.

No one spoke for a good fifteen minutes. Mike's phone broke into the silence and he pulled it out of his pocket and handed it to Dana since Mitch was in the back seat. She hit the speaker button. "Hello?"

"It's me," Noah said. "I have the SUV and the shoe box with the Glock is still beneath the seat. I'll catch up with you guys soon."

"Great, thanks for letting us know." Dana disconnected from the call and handed the phone back to Mitch's brother. "I'm relieved the gun is still there."

"Me, too." Mitch reached for her hand and she savored the way his fingers cradled hers. Then he rested his head against the cushion and closed his eyes.

The ride to Stilton took almost an hour, partially because they hit the height of rush hour going through downtown Milwaukee. When Dana saw the billboard advertising The Sandpiper Motel, she gently shook Mitch awake.

"We'll be there soon," she said, when he groggily looked at her.

"Okay." He grimaced and put a hand over his stomach.

She frowned. "Do you feel sick?"

"A little. Could be the meds."

"Or the fact that we haven't eaten anything since breakfast and it's dinnertime." Dana caught Mike's gaze in the mirror. "Can we stop for something to eat?"

"Of course. What are you in the mood for?"

Mitch shrugged. "Nothing heavy, that's for sure. Maybe soup and toast."

"Karen's Kitchen is our best option," Dana said.

Mike nodded. "Seems reasonable. I'll let Noah know where we are."

When Mike parked at the restaurant, Mitch was able to get out of the car without help. She hoped that he'd feel even better once he'd gotten something to eat.

The three of them sat in a booth, Mitch and Dana on one side, with Mike across from them. The place was busy, but the servers did a good job of keeping up. Within five minutes they were given water and had their orders placed.

Mike made the call to Noah letting him know where

they were. Noah was stuck in the same traffic they'd been in, only worse because of a car accident shutting down the interstate.

When their food arrived, Dana looked at Mitch, then instinctively bowed her head for his mealtime prayer.

"Dear Lord, thank You for providing this food we are about to eat," Mitch began. "Please continue to guide us on Your chosen path as we seek justice against those who have harmed others. We ask this in Your holy name. Amen."

"Amen," Dana and Mike echoed.

"And we ask that You continue to keep Dana and Mitch safe, as well," Mike added. "Amen."

Dana was startled at how Mike included her and realized that both Callahan brothers were treating her as family, the same way they'd welcomed Noah.

She suddenly understood that it wasn't a structure that made a home, but having people who cared about you.

And now that she'd experienced what her life could be like, she had no intention of going back to the dull, listless way she'd existed before.

Mitch ate gingerly, taking a few sips of chicken noodle soup along with a bite of toast. His stomach didn't rebel, which he took as a good sign.

"Doing okay?" Dana asked, her green eyes full of concern.

"Yeah." He reached over and gently squeezed her hand. "Thanks."

Her gaze dropped. "I'm the one who needs to thank you for saving my life."

"Hey." He brought her hand up to lightly brush a kiss against her knuckles. "We're in this together, okay?"

She attempted a smile. "I know. It's just...we don't know much more than when we first escaped the knife guy at the hospital."

"True." He couldn't deny that they didn't have much to show for all their investigating.

"Not true," Mike countered. "We know your former partner, Jeff, was paid off by Shelton, Inc. to deem the fires on their properties due to natural causes. We know that Mitch has been targeted because he made it clear the fire was the result of arson, so he needed to be discredited."

"Those are theories, not facts," Mitch pointed out.

"Okay, maybe you're right. However, your being framed for murder is a fact and the only reason that makes sense is because you took over Jeff's cases after his death. And Jeff's notes show that he investigated several fires belonging to Shelton, Inc., and they were all determined to be accidental."

He couldn't disagree with Mike's point. "So why is Dana in danger?"

Mike took a bite of his burger, chewed and swallowed. "I don't know. But I sense that once we answer that million-dollar question, we'll know who's ultimately behind all of this."

After they finished eating, Mike paid the bill and they headed back outside. When they arrived at the motel, Mitch went inside to request the same two rooms they used previously.

Suzy, the young college student behind the counter, remembered him, and gave him the keys in exchange for cash without a fuss.

"Drive around back," Mitch said.

Mike did as instructed, pulling up in front of the door to the room Mitch had used earlier. He gave Dana her key, and within minutes they met at the connecting door.

"Noah will be here shortly," Mike said, slipping his phone into his pocket. "Anything else you need before we go?"

He swept a gaze over the familiar room. "Assuming Jeff's notes are still in the SUV, along with the laptop computer, nothing I can think of."

Mike nodded and took up a position near the window so he could see the parking lot. Mitch stretched out on the bed, grateful for a chance to rest. The events of the day were catching up with him, and he wasn't 100 percent sure that the drugs were fully flushed from his system, either.

The minutes passed by slowly until Mike abruptly straightened. "He's here."

Mitch swung his legs over the edge of the bed and sat up. Dana watched him intently, as if expecting him to pass out at her feet. The room spun for a moment and he focused on staying upright, proving her wrong.

"I think this is everything," Mike said, dropping the laptop on the table along with the file folder of notes. Noah brought in the shoe box containing the Glock.

"Thanks." Mitch was grateful his brothers had his back.

"Hold on." Mike snagged Noah's arm. "It might be better for us to hang on to the murder weapon."

Mitch scowled. "Why? I was considering picking up ammo for it, just in case we're ambushed again."

"If you need a weapon, I'll let you borrow mine," Noah said. "Using the Glock will only add to the evidence against you."

"He's right," Mike said. "I'd feel better if you weren't connected to the Glock at all."

"I'm not *connected* to it," Mitch said, with a flash of irritation. "The stupid thing was planted in my closet by the real killer."

"All the more reason you shouldn't have it in your possession," Mike said calmly. "Noah, you can't give up your service weapon. If Mitch has to use it, you could lose your job."

Mitch grimaced. He didn't want to put his brother-in-law's career in jeopardy any more than he had already. "Mike's right. I'm sure we'll be fine."

"You can borrow mine." Mike lifted his pant leg, showing his ankle holster. He removed the small thirty-eight and holster, handing them both over to Mitch. "Don't use it unless you absolutely have to."

"I won't," Mitch promised, bending over to strap the holster to his own ankle. Truthfully, he hated the idea of using the weapon, but after the near miss with the tranquilizer gun, he wasn't going to take any chances.

"We'll call you if we learn anything more," Noah said as he and Mike turned toward the door. "Stay safe."

"Will do." Mitch pushed himself to his feet, so he could lock the door behind them. Then he dropped into the seat at the table and booted up the computer.

"This isn't the time for that, you need some rest," Dana protested.

She was right, but he didn't move, unable to get rid of the nagging feeling that he was missing something.

Something obvious.

But what?

He searched again on Shelton, Inc. The same sites came up that he'd looked at before. The words blurred on the screen and he rubbed his palms over his eyes in an attempt to clear them. It didn't help.

Reluctantly, he was forced to admit that no matter how much he wanted to keep working, his body needed rest.

"I'll look at this later," he said, closing the computer. "After a quick power nap."

"You'd better take your antibiotic." Dana opened the small white bag the ER nurse had given them. "And I'd like to take a peek at your incision."

He downed the antibiotic horse pill and chased it with water, hoping it wasn't what had made him feel sick. He turned his head to the right so that Dana could peer at his neck incision. Her lilac scent washed over him, bringing a stab of guilt.

"I'm sorry," he said in a low tone. "I should have sent Mike and Noah to Simon's apartment building. Instead, I risked your life. I hope you can forgive me."

"Oh, Mitch." Dana bent over and placed a chaste kiss on his cheek. "Of course. After all, you saved my life by taking the dart intended for me."

"You returned the favor by staying nearby until Mike could rescue us." He wanted nothing more than to pull her close and kiss her properly.

Maybe his longing was evident in his eyes, because Dana slowly bent forward a second time, this time lightly brushing her mouth against his. Once. Twice.

"Dana," he groaned and pulled her closer, deepening the kiss.

She tasted like summer, sweetness and rain. He didn't want to let her go, but eventually needed to breathe. This time, Dana didn't immediately move away, but gulped air, too, letting him know she enjoyed the kiss as much as he had.

He wanted to see her again, once this nightmare was over, but it occurred to him that even if they found a suspect, it still might take months to clear his name.

And he had no right to ask any woman, least of all Dana, to wait for him. Especially since, for all he knew, he didn't even have a job any longer. Or a life outside of prison.

"I—um, need some sleep," he said, inching away from her. "Thanks, Dana."

She looked confused, then embarrassed. "Of course. Let me know if you need anything else."

"Dana." He caught her hand before she could bolt away. "I care about you. If we get caught, I'll do everything in my power to protect your name and reputation."

"And I'll do everything in my power to prove your innocence," she countered. "So let's just not get caught, okay?"

He couldn't help but smile. "Okay."

Dana edged around him to head through the connecting door. Mitch once again stretched out on the bed and closed his eyes, relaxing into the mattress with relief.

Just an hour, he thought as he drifted to sleep.

The muffled thud of a car door had him bolting upright, all senses on high alert. The sun was low in the sky, which meant he'd slept longer than he'd planned.

"Is someone out there?" Dana whispered.

He moved toward the window to scan the parking lot. When he caught a glimpse of the guy's profile, he recoiled from the window.

"I think it's the same guy who was sitting and watching my house," he whispered.

"What should we do?"

"You take cover in your room." Mitch considered the gun on his ankle for a nanosecond, then discarded the idea. Instead he picked up one of the heavy wooden chairs and stood behind the door. "Hurry," he hissed.

Dana looked indecisive for a moment, but then they

heard the sound of the key card being used to unlock his motel room door. The guy must have convinced Suzy to give him a duplicate.

Dana melted back behind the connecting door, swinging it closed at the same time the guy entered the room, gun held at the ready.

Mitch waited one beat, then another. The guy took another step farther into the room and that's when he made his move, bringing the chair down hard on the intruder's head and outstretched arm.

The man pitched forward, crumpling to the floor.

The motel room door shut with a loud click.

Dana ran forward, kicking the weapon away from the guy's outstretched hand. Then she bent down to feel for a pulse.

"He's still alive," she said in relief.

"Let's get out of here, but through your room, not mine." He grabbed the computer, file folder and car keys from the table. Stepping over the prone figure on the floor, he crossed the threshold into Dana's room.

"Wait…" Dana protested. At first he thought she was going to continue to offer first aid to the guy, but then smiled in grim approval as she picked up his gun, holding it gingerly by the barrel as if she didn't trust herself not to shoot it off by accident. "Okay, got it."

He cracked the door of her room and scanned the parking lot to see if anyone else might be lurking outside.

There! A second man, wearing a baseball hat pulled low over his brow, was approaching Mitch's motel room door. Knife guy? Did he have a key, too? Mitch had to assume so. Yes. The moment the guy accessed the motel room, stepping inside, he urged Dana forward.

"Run," he whispered.

They bolted for the SUV. The guy inside the motel room came running back out, shooting wildly.

What was with these guys? "Keep your head down," he said, stomping on the gas. The SUV shot forward, and he drove as fast as he dared, putting distance between them and the motel.

It wasn't until they were far from the motel that he wondered how in the world they'd been found at The Sandpiper.

Was there anywhere they could go to stay safe?

FOURTEEN

Clutching the gun in her lap, Dana took deep breaths in an attempt to slow her racing heart.

How had the two gunmen found them?

She felt guilty for leaving an injured man behind, but hoped the second man would get the hurt man the help he needed.

"Call Mike," Mitch said, tossing her the cell phone. "Let him know The Sandpiper has been compromised."

She carefully put the gun in the glove compartment, then picked up the phone. Her fingers shook with adrenaline as she made the call using the speaker function so Mitch could hear. The phone rang for what seemed like forever before Mike picked up. "Hello?"

"It's Dana and Mitch. Two gunmen found us at the motel."

"What?" Mike sounded incredulous. "How?"

"That's what I'm trying to figure out," Mitch said. "One of the guys looked familiar, I think he was the cop sitting outside my house and the second guy was wearing a baseball cap just like the guy who'd attempted to stab me in the ER. The knife guy must be working with the cop. Noah ran the license plate number for me."

"I remember," Mike agreed. "He told me the number

came back as belonging to a guy named Calvin Towne who works for the MPD."

"Were they there to arrest Mitch?" Dana asked.

"No. The normal arrest routine doesn't include two men approaching a fugitive on their own." Mike was silent for a moment. "I'll ask Noah to dig further into that license plate."

"Thanks." Mitch's expression was grim. "I'll find a new place for us to stay."

"Listen, Mitch, don't tell anyone where you end up, okay?" Mike's tone was serious. "Including me and Noah."

Dana frowned. "Why not?"

"Somehow we must have slipped up along the way." Mike was silent for a long moment. "I'm not sure how, but there's no other explanation."

A shiver of fear rippled down her spine. How would they find a way out of this mess without Mike and Noah's help?

"You don't know that for sure," Mitch said. "Could be Suzy the college student recognized me from a news story and decided to call it in to the MPD."

"Maybe, but not likely. If the MPD knew where you were, they would have come with a full team since you're considered armed and dangerous."

Dana's stomach knotted at the idea of a full SWAT team arriving at the motel. She didn't have personal experience, just the stuff she saw on TV, but she knew there was always the possibility a cop might shoot first and ask questions later.

"Stay safe," Mike said. "I'll let you know if we come up with anything on the license plate."

"Thanks," Mitch said.

Dana ended the call and set Mitch's phone in the cup

holder in the center console. Outside it was full-on dark, and the bright lights of oncoming traffic from the other side of the highway made her look away.

"Keep your eyes out for another place to stay," Mitch said in a terse voice.

"All right." She could tell Mitch was upset, and she didn't blame him. They'd managed to escape several times now, but how long could they evade the men searching for them?

"I'd drop you off at the nearest police station if I could," he said. "But you're in danger, too. And I don't know who we can trust."

"I trust you." The words were instinctive and true. "We'll get through this, Mitch, you'll see."

He nodded, but didn't say anything more. They drove for miles and miles until they passed by the small town of Kearney. She caught a glimpse of a neon vacancy sign. "Did you see that?" she asked. "We just passed a motel."

Mitch nodded, and made several turns, doubling back to the small motel. It was off the beaten track, which she thought was probably good. The vacancy sign had caught her eye mostly because she was looking for a place, and there hadn't been any billboards advertising it, either.

When Mitch pulled up in front of the small motel, she put a hand on his arm to prevent him from getting out of the car. "Let me go in. Your face might be too recognizable."

He scowled but then nodded. "Okay." He dug in his back pocket and handed her a wad of cash. "I'll wait here."

Dana slipped out of the SUV and headed inside. The clerk was an elderly man who might have been hard of hearing because he didn't move or glance at her until she was right up to the desk.

"Need a room?" he asked in a booming voice.

She smiled. "Two, please. Connecting rooms if you have them."

"Got a passel of kids, do ya?" The old man cackled at his own joke.

She forced a smile, trying not to remember the baby she'd lost. "How much?"

He named his price so she peeled off the bills, pushing the cash across the counter. He frowned. "I prefer credit cards."

"I'm sorry, I shredded them." She shrugged. "Please?"

"Fine." The old man relented, taking the cash and pushing two key cards toward her.

It wasn't until she was safely back outside that she let out her breath in a relieved whoosh. She opened the door and climbed in, showing Mitch the keys. "We're all set. Rooms nine and ten on the end."

"Good." Mitch drove past the lobby and parked in front of room nine. "Take the computer inside. I'm going to find a place to park the SUV where it's not in view of the street."

She handed him the key to room ten, picked up the computer and the file folder and headed into the motel. The rooms weren't as bad as she'd expected—not great, but not awful. Good enough for what was left of the night.

It seemed to take Mitch a long time to return. She peered out the window, nearly jumping out of her skin when she saw a male figure standing in front of room ten. Mitch entered the room, then opened his side of the connecting door.

"How far did you go?" she asked. "I was getting worried."

"There's a truck stop about a mile down the road. I left the SUV there and walked back."

"I see." She wasn't sure if it was a good idea to have their vehicle so far away from the motel. "Hopefully we won't need to leave in a hurry."

Mike dropped into a chair with a heavy sigh. "There are a few ways we could have been found at The Sandpiper. Suzy recognized me and turned me in. The guy sitting outside my house managed to figure out I was using Hawk's SUV and got a tip it was there earlier. Or Mike was followed. My goal was to eliminate all possibilities of being found a second time."

"Suzy turning you in seems the most likely."

Mitch shook his head. "I don't know, maybe. But as Mike pointed out, if the MPD knew I was there, they would have come in with a large fugitive apprehension team. Not two guys carrying nothing but handguns."

"Yeah, I noticed they didn't have tranquilizer guns," she said thoughtfully. "I wonder if they gave up on that idea."

"That's what I'm thinking," Mitch agreed. "Two strikes and you're out, right? Then it's onto a different plan."

Being targeted by someone who wanted her dead was still a difficult concept to grasp. Her life, before she saw Mitch's name on the ER census board, had been nothing but dull, boring and routine.

So why would anyone target her?

"Are you okay?" Mitch asked.

She glanced up and met his intent gaze. "Yes."

"Quick thinking, kicking the gun out of the way and

bringing it with us," he said. "In the morning, I'll call Noah, see if he can get fingerprints off it."

She brightened at that thought. So far they'd had nothing much to go on. Identifying even one of the men involved could help point them in the right direction.

Mitch scrubbed his hands over his face. "I know I'm missing something."

"It does seem odd that there are more planted clues pointing at you being the murderer than we've been able to uncover about anyone else."

"I know." Mitch blew out a heavy breath. "I keep coming back to Simon's muddy work boots. Maybe we need to look for a connection between construction companies and Shelton, Inc."

"Shelton, Inc. is a construction company, isn't it? At least, that's what Kent claimed."

"Not exactly." Mitch opened the computer and waited for it to connect to the motel Wi-Fi. "They owned the warehouses, but I believe they were listed as a property management company, not a construction business."

She moved to sit beside Mitch so she could see the computer screen, too. "There have to be dozens of construction companies out there."

"You can say that again," Mitch muttered. He scrolled down the list on the screen. "Everything from Amstar Building Corporation to Zacharias Construction. Not to mention about twenty other companies in between."

A name caught her eye. "Wait, what is that one? Worth More Construction?"

"Yeah. What about it?"

Dana raised her gaze to his. "That's the name of the company that built the house."

He frowned. "You mean the one Kent's parents bought for you and Kent as a wedding gift?"

She nodded slowly, a sick feeling settling in the pit of her stomach. "It was originally a model house, used as a showcase for others."

"Are the other houses in your neighborhood also Worth More homes?"

She nodded. Then it hit her. Kent's full name. "Kentworth," she said abruptly. "Do you think it's possible that the name Worth More is a coincidence?"

Mitch didn't answer, but clicked on the link. A webpage came up displaying beautiful homes.

Exactly like the one she was living in.

Were Kent's parents owners of Worth More Construction?

And if so, why were there so many layers of companies with different names?

What exactly did it all mean?

Finally something to go on. Mitch could barely contain his excitement. "Maybe Simon was working for Worth More Construction on his off days. Kent must have gotten him the job as a way to help him make ends meet."

"We don't know for sure Kent's parents are involved," Dana protested.

"They are. I don't believe in coincidences." He dug into the Worth More Construction name, trying to drill down to the ownership level.

It wasn't easy.

Should he call Mike for assistance? Glancing at his watch, he realized it was well past one o'clock in the morning. Granted, he had gotten a little sleep earlier, but exhaustion still pulled at him. Might be better to wait until morning. They could check for fingerprints on the gun and dig into the ownership of Worth More Construction.

"Can't find it?" Dana asked, hiding a yawn.

"No." He closed the computer. "Mike will help us tomorrow. For now, let's get some sleep."

"All right."

Since he was in her room, he left the computer behind and headed through the connecting door. He wished he could shower, but knew he still couldn't get the sutures wet, so he settled for a quick washup in the bathroom.

Mindful of the way they'd been found before, he unhooked the ankle holster and set it on the bedside table, close at hand.

He dreamed of the night Kent died. Beating the fire back with the hose, feeling as if they were making progress until a loud explosion shook the building. A severe back draft of fire surging around them. Kent panicking as smoke filled the inside of his mask. Kent ripping the mask off, coughing as he inhaled smoke and soot, then collapsing onto the floor. Mitch grabbing him, slinging him over his shoulder and hauling him out of the burning building.

Round after round of CPR as he tried to revive the rookie.

Then being pulled off him as the paramedics arrived, declaring him DOA.

No!

Mitch awoke with a start, heart pounding so ferociously he was surprised it didn't crack his ribs. He blinked, surprised to see early-morning light streaming in from the narrow opening in the curtain hanging over the window.

He rose and headed into the bathroom to splash cold

water on his face. It had been a long time since he'd dreamed of that night. At least two years, maybe more.

At the time he had insisted that Kent's gear be checked out for a possible malfunction, but Kent had dropped it inside and the fire had burned it beyond recognition.

Lifting his head, he stared at his ragged reflection in the mirror. Despite rigorous training, it wasn't unheard of for a rookie to panic during the real deal. There wasn't any reason to suspect foul play.

In fact, he had sensed Kent's immaturity. It was one of the reasons he'd wanted the rookie to stay outside to man the hoses.

But what if he was wrong? What if Kent's death wasn't an accident?

He shook his head at his ridiculous thoughts. Even if he had questions surrounding Kent's death, it didn't matter at this late date. Three years had passed. What had happened back then didn't have anything to do with the here and now.

His cell phone rang. Mitch crossed the room to pick it up, recognizing his brother's number. "Hey, Mike. What's up?"

"I've got good news and bad news," his brother said in a weary tone.

"Give me the bad news first," Mitch said. Dana poked her head through the connecting door and he waved her in. He put the call on speaker so she could listen in.

"MPD has staked out my place and Noah's," Mike said. "We ended up staying in a motel here in town to avoid being detained."

"I'm sorry to hear that." Mitch closed his eyes and

rubbed at the spot between his eyebrows. "What's the good news?"

"The license plate you saw on the car parked outside your house does belong to the MPD, but it's been reported stolen."

"Are you kidding me? That's the good news?" His voice rose in agitation. "That means we're no closer to finding out who's behind all this."

"You didn't let me finish," Mike said. "Noah was able to find out that Calvin Towne has a brother-in-law who apparently works as a security guard for…guess who? Shelton, Inc."

Mitch dropped onto the edge of the bed in shocked surprise. "What's his name?"

"Tyler Pitrowski. Ring any bells?"

He glanced at Dana, who grimaced and shook her head. "Nope. Doesn't sound familiar to either of us. Although Dana picked up the guy's gun at the motel. It's in my glove compartment. If we can match the fingerprints to this Tyler Pitrowski guy, then we'll know for sure."

"Told you I had good news." Mike sounded smug.

"A connection to Shelton, Inc. is good news," Mitch agreed. "Reinforces our theory that Jeff must have been taking payoffs on the side to benefit Shelton, Inc."

"That's what we thought," Mike said. "Glad to hear you have the guy's gun in your possession, too. We need all the evidence of you being framed we can get."

No joke. "I need some additional help, bro," he said. "There may be a connection between Shelton, Inc. Property Management and a builder by the name of Worth More Construction. Can you find out who owns Worth More?"

"Sure." Mitch could hear Mike tapping keys on a computer. "Why do you think they're linked?"

"Because Kent's full name is Kentworth," Dana said, speaking up for the first time. "And the house that was given to us as a wedding gift by Kent's parents was built by Worth More Construction."

Mike let out a low whistle. "Very interesting. Okay, but this is going to take some time, so I'll call you back."

"Thanks, bro. I owe you more than I'll ever be able to repay."

"I'll figure out a way to collect, don't worry. Later." Mike disconnected from the call.

"We're going to figure it all out, aren't we?" Dana asked, her expression hopeful. "It's finally coming together."

He didn't want to burst her bubble, but the truth was, they could find all the connections in the world, but without proof? They were nowhere.

Especially considering all the evidence that they'd planted against him.

"Mitch?" Dana's voice was tentative. "We are close to figuring this all out, aren't we?"

He forced a confident smile. "Yeah. Enough for reasonable doubt, for sure."

She frowned. "Are you saying you'll still have to go to trial?"

"Depends. But regardless, it's nothing to worry about right now. Are you hungry? I can hike to the truck stop to pick up the SUV."

"Maybe we should both go. I'd rather not stay here alone."

He hesitated, then nodded. "Okay." It wouldn't be that big of a deal to carry their stuff. He shut down the computer, tucked the file folder inside and picked it up. Dana disappeared into her room, returning with the small white bag containing his antibiotic and dressing supplies.

"Stay on my left," he instructed. He was right-handed, needing his body to be between Dana and anyone traveling on the road. It didn't seem possible that they'd been followed last night; there hadn't been another car behind them for miles.

But he hadn't planned on being found at The Sandpiper, either.

"Should we find a different motel in another town after breakfast?" Dana asked.

"Yeah." He knew that this running around from motel to motel couldn't go on forever. Eventually they would run out of cash. "Although if Mike uncovers something, we can meet up with him first to hand over the thirty-eight."

She nodded. "This whole thing reminds me of that old Harrison Ford movie *The Fugitive*. He was framed for murder, just like you."

He didn't answer since this felt more real than a movie. Although he couldn't deny there were parallels.

As they approached the truck stop, Mitch swept his gaze around the area, looking for signs of trouble. He didn't see anything unusual, so he unlocked the SUV and stored the computer and file folder inside. Then he took Dana's hand as they went into the diner.

The truck stop was busy, but they managed to snag the last empty booth. Breakfast smells, especially bacon, filled the air, and he was grateful when their server provided two cups of steaming coffee.

After they placed their order, Mitch took a careful survey of the people in the restaurant. Mostly men, although the occasional older couple as well, maybe locals from the area. He and Dana were the youngest and he hoped they wouldn't attract too much attention.

It didn't take long for their breakfast to arrive, and he was surprised when Dana reached over to take his hand. He smiled and said grace, giving her fingers an encouraging squeeze before letting go.

As they finished their breakfast, his phone rang again, displaying Mike's number, and this time he didn't put it on speaker, not wanting anyone to overhear. "You found something?" he asked.

"Yeah. You were right. Worth More Construction is owned by ASP, Inc., which is a subsidiary of Shelton, Inc."

"ASP?" he repeated.

The color drained from Dana's face. "Alice Shelton Petrie," she whispered. "Kent's mother."

Mitch repeated the information for Mike's benefit. Another piece of the puzzle fell into place.

"We need to understand the motive here," he said to Mike. "This all has to be connected in some way."

"I'll keep digging."

Mitch didn't answer right away. He was starting to believe that the only way to find out the truth would be to get it directly from the people involved.

Alice and Edward Petrie.

FIFTEEN

Dana wasn't sure what Alice's role in all of this was, but the thread stretching between all the companies couldn't be denied.

"Thanks, Mike. Let me know if you find anything else. I'll call you back when we're settled in someplace new."

"He's going to keep investigating?" she asked.

Mitch nodded, signaling for the bill.

She pushed her plate away and picked up her coffee. "I think I should call Kent's parents."

"No." Mitch's refusal was curt. "I don't want you in danger."

She leaned forward, keeping her voice down. "I can't believe they would hurt me and we need to find out what's really going on."

Mitch didn't answer right away, but waited for their server to bring the bill. He left cash on the table, then slid out of the booth, offering his hand.

She took it and followed him outside. Dark clouds covered the sky, indicating a storm was moving in. Mike's rented SUV was parked in a corner facing forward. Mitch opened the door for her, helped her in and then slid in behind the wheel.

"We'll find another place to stay, then call Mike back," he said breaking the silence. "We need more to go on before we risk contacting the Petries."

She didn't necessarily agree, but figured waiting a few more hours wouldn't hurt.

Mitch drove headed south and east to the opposite side of the city. Thankfully, they found another small motel that advertised Wi-Fi services. Once again, Dana went in to obtain their rooms so that Mitch remained in the SUV, hidden from view.

The owners of the motel were an elderly couple who didn't ask any questions and accepted cash without blinking an eye.

Once they were settled in the rooms, Mitch opened the computer. She took the seat next to him so she could see, as well.

The first thing he did was access the Wisconsin Circuit Court database. He typed in the name Tyler Pitrowski. The last name was unusual enough that there was only one guy in the database, who had several charges for drug possession and one felony charge with intent to sell.

"Drugs?" She frowned. "That doesn't seem like it would be connected to the arson fires."

Mitch shrugged. "I think it's even stranger that Shelton, Inc., would hire a security guard with a criminal record. Wouldn't they do a background check?"

"Does the database say what kind of drugs?" she asked.

"No." Mitch paused. "Why does it matter?"

Dana sighed. "I keep going back to the dart guns laced with carfentanil, the most dangerous narcotic ever made. And the fact that it's only recently been showing up on the streets. I can't help but wonder if there's a connection between the drugs and the warehouse fires."

"That's something to consider," Mitch agreed. He reached for his phone to call Mike.

"Put it on speaker," Dana said.

He did. After two rings, Mike picked up. "Hey, I was just going to call you. I found out more information."

"Tell us," Mitch urged.

"It's a little complicated, but here's what I found by digging into the fire prior to this most recent one. There's a company called Chicago Land Corp. They actually sold the warehouse to ASP, Inc. for half a million."

Mitch let out a low whistle. "That's a lot of money for a warehouse."

"I know, right? Especially since the value of the property isn't even close to that amount. The land is only valued at one hundred thousand dollars. After the fire, the insurance company reimbursed ASP, Inc. for the full value. And then ASP, Inc. put the property on the market for the normal land value of one hundred thousand."

Dana frowned as Mitch scribbled the numbers on a blank sheet of paper. "So you're saying that ASP, Inc. is making out on the deal by earning an extra hundred grand?"

"At the very least. But it could be they're making even more on the deal," Mike said. "I haven't been able to track down the original owners of Chicago Land Corp. It's as if they don't exist outside of paper."

Dana still wasn't sure she understood. "So what?"

"Hear me out. Why would anyone buy a property that's overvalued in the first place?"

"No clue," Mitch said.

"I think they're buying these buildings from an underground organization for the actual cost of the property, say one hundred grand, but put a higher price on paper so they can justify the insurance coverage. They start construction, then there's a fire. Once the fire is accidental in nature, the insurance company pays out the full half million. Then, instead of rebuilding, they sell the property for the cost they actually purchased it for, the original one hundred grand."

"That's an interesting theory, bro, but we can't prove it."

"I know," Mike agreed. "I'm still working on finding more about Chicago Land Corp. But once I found the details of the fire from a few months ago, I thought I'd start digging into the most recent one. So far, I have a similar paper trail. The property was allegedly purchased for four hundred and fifty thousand dollars from Chicago Land Corp. Only difference is that the buyer is Shelton, Inc. instead of ASP, Inc. I believe they're using different subsidiary companies so that they don't attract attention."

"And it would have worked," Mitch said, "if I hadn't taken over Jeff's cases and deemed the source of the fire as arson."

"Exactly." Satisfaction rang in Mike's tone. "This is why they're trying to discredit you. Especially if you're able to go back through Jeff's notes and overrule his previous investigations, too."

Dana couldn't deny there was logic in Mike's assessment. "But how does this help us, moving forward? How are we going to be able to prove Mitch is being set up for murder?"

"That's a good question," Mike said. "Maybe I'll keep looking for other properties that Shelton, Inc.,

Worth More Construction and ASP, Inc. own. Maybe they already have another potential fire in the works."

"That's a great idea," Mitch agreed. "Oh, and Dana has a theory about illegal drugs being part of the mix."

"What do you mean?"

Dana was surprised Mitch had brought it up to his brother. "It's the carfentanil that was found in Mitch's bloodstream," she said. "It just seems odd to have the drug connected to the men who are trying to kill us. I'm wondering if the Chicago-based company uses these warehouses as a place to manufacture drugs, then when they feel the places outlive their usefulness, they sell the properties to Shelton, Inc."

There was a long moment of silence before Mike said, "I guess anything is possible."

"What we need is to check out one of the current warehouses owned by Chicago Land Corp.," Mitch said. "Maybe that's where we'll find the proof we need."

"I'll do my best," Mike said. "Are you guys someplace safe?"

"Yeah." Mitch didn't elaborate further. "Call me back if you find something."

"Will do."

Mitch pushed the end button, then sat back in his chair, gesturing to his notes. "What do you think of Mike's theory?"

"I hate thinking of Kent's parents being involved in anything illegal," she said. "I mean yes, they're rich and stuffy, but they truly loved Kent. Why would they risk everything for money when they're already well-off?"

"The real estate market crashed ten years ago," Mitch mused. "Maybe they took a hit during that time and needed to make up the difference."

"Maybe." She couldn't deny his point.

"Did Kent leave any paperwork behind about the house you're currently living in?"

"What kind of paperwork?"

"Anything about the value of the house, when it was built, who the subcontractors were."

Dana slowly shook her head. "Kent's parents have all of that information." She looked up and met Mitch's gaze. "But now that I know they built the place, it's strange how upset they get when I mention moving out of the house into something smaller."

"Who would get the house if something happened to you?" Mitch asked.

"I've listed them as the beneficiaries," she said with a shrug. "At the time it seemed logical. I wouldn't have the house at all if it wasn't for them giving it to us as a wedding gift."

"Your name is on the title?"

She nodded. "Yes, but I still don't believe the attempts on my life are related to the house. It makes no sense. Why not simply offer me a low price? They have to know I'd take it."

"But with you out of the picture, they get the property at full value."

"I don't believe it." She rose to her feet and walked over to the window overlooking the highway. The sidewalk was damp with rain.

She'd known Kent's parents for several years. It didn't make sense that they'd try to hurt her now. What had changed? Nothing.

Everything. She'd met Mitch Callahan and had started actually living her life instead of existing. But would the Petries know that?

And even if they did, why had they fought her idea of

selling the place? She'd assumed they wanted her living there as a way of clinging to Kent's memory.

What if she was wrong? She rested her forehead on the glass for a long moment, then abruptly straightened, swinging around to face Mitch.

Maybe it was related to her being with Mitch. There hadn't been an attempt on her life until after she'd helped him escape from the knife guy in the ER.

Was it possible that rescuing Mitch had caused the Petries to turn against her? Why not? If the Petries were raking insurance companies for money from fires on their property, maybe they decided to take her and Mitch out at the same time.

Eliminating both problems in one fell swoop.

"Something wrong?" Mitch didn't like the shocked expression in Dana's eyes.

"I just can't believe Kent's parents would do all this—" she gestured helplessly in the air "—for money. It's a crazy, complicated scheme."

Mitch had been thinking along the same lines. "Almost seems easier to kill us outright and be done with it."

She shivered and rubbed her hands over her arms. "Yes."

"Although maybe after Jeff's death, they thought it would be better to frame me than to kill me."

Her expression was pained. "Can we stop talking about being killed? It's unsettling."

He crossed over and gently pulled her into his arms. "I'll keep you safe, Dana."

She rested her cheek against his chest. "I know. But it's already been several days. How much longer can we live like this?"

He didn't have a good answer for her.

"If we get out of this…" she began.

"When," he interrupted, pressing a kiss to her temple. "Let's think positive. When we get out of this."

He could feel her smile and decided to count that as a victory. "When we get out of this, I'm moving out of Kent's house. In fact, I'd rather not go back there ever again."

"Understandable," he replied. "We'll only go back long enough to pack your things, okay?"

"Okay." She wrapped her arms around his waist and hugged him. "Thanks, Mitch."

He didn't deserve her gratitude. "I'm the reason you're in this mess."

"Not really." She leaned back so she could look up at him. "Since Kent's death, I've only been existing, not living my life." A smile tipped the corners of her mouth. "Until I came over to talk to you. And now that I've begun to enjoy life, I don't think I'll be able to go back to the way it was before."

"I'm glad." His voice was low and husky and it was taking everything he had not to kiss her again. "You deserve to be happy."

Her smile faded. "I haven't felt happy in a long time. But now, with you, it feels right."

His heart soared with joy and he stopped fighting his instincts. Slowly, giving her a chance to pull away, he lowered his mouth to hers.

She met his kiss with one of her own and he gathered her close, wishing they could stay like this, cocooned from the world forever.

Then he wasn't thinking at all, only feeling.

The shrill ringing of his phone finally broke them apart, and even then he was mentally cursing his brother's rotten timing. Reluctantly he eased her aside so he could grab the stupid phone.

"What?" He didn't care if he sounded crabby.

"What's the matter, I interrupt you again?"

"Knock it off," he growled, glancing at Dana. "If you have news, I'll put you on speaker."

"I have news." Mike waited for a minute while Mitch pressed the speaker button, then continued, "I found another warehouse that is currently owned by Chicago Land Corp."

Mitch felt a surge of anticipation. "Where?"

"Downtown Milwaukee, in the old manufacturing district just off Riverbend Street. Chicago Land Corp. has owned it for about three months. Figured we could check out Dana's theory, see if there's any link to the drug trade."

"I'd like to go along," Dana said.

Mitch instinctively wanted to protest, but his brother did it for him. "I'm not sure that's a good idea," Mike said. "Better for you and Mitch to stay where you are."

"What I've learned about street drugs from working in the ER might be helpful. We've been educated especially on carfentanil."

"We need all the help we can get," Mitch pointed out. "And we should head out soon, take advantage of the crummy weather."

"Yeah, okay," Mike relented. "Let's meet at a neutral place, say outside the Brat Stop."

Their old familiar stomping grounds made Mitch grin. "Give us twenty minutes and we'll see you there."

"Sounds good."

Mitch tucked the phone into his pocket and then shut down the computer. Dana came over to help put their notes back into the file folders. Their fingers brushed, causing an electrical jolt to shimmy up his arm.

It occurred to him that he hadn't had this kind of chemistry with Janice. Was this what his brothers and Maddy had experienced when they'd found their mates? If so, he should be grateful he'd found out about Janice and Simon.

In less than two minutes, they were back in the rented SUV. The sky was so dark he needed to use his headlights to see through the rain.

Mitch had a good feeling about this lead on the warehouse and wondered if Shelton, Inc., was already in the process of purchasing the place.

Now that he thought about it, the fires Jeff had investigated had been spaced at least five months apart. So maybe the sale wouldn't be in the works for another few months.

"Is that the Brat Stop?" Dana asked, peering through the rain. "I'm surprised it's busy with this weather."

"Good news for us, an extra car in the lot won't be noticed." He pulled into the parking lot and spied Hawk's SUV. The water had washed away the mud from the license plate. Using his phone, he dialed Mike. "We need to take the rental."

"Be right there." Mike opened the door and ran through the rain to meet them. "Good thing it's warm out," his brother groused from the back seat.

"We won't melt." Mitch glanced over his shoulder. "What's the address?"

"Corner of Riverbend and Morgan."

Mitch nodded, recognizing the area. He put the car in gear and then drove out of the Brat Stop parking lot.

"Let's do a drive-by first," Mike suggested. "See if there's any sign of activity."

"Sure." Mitch kept his eyes on the road, aware of the slick surface.

"Dana, what do you know about this new narcotic?" Mike asked.

"It's usurping heroin because there's a higher payoff for the drug suppliers. A small amount goes a long way and it's cheaper to manufacture. And it can even be absorbed through skin, and of course mucous membranes like your nose and mouth." Dana shook her head. "But it's also causing deaths, which is counterproductive to the drug trade."

"Do you know how it's made?" Mike asked.

"I don't know exactly but I know it's man-made and can be created in a lab, much like meth."

"Perfect use for a warehouse," Mitch muttered. "Is that it up ahead?"

"Slow down," Mike directed. "I think it's the old gray building at the end of the street."

At first he thought the place was abandoned. But then he saw the faint beam of light from a window along the side of the building.

"Someone's in there," he said.

"Yeah, I saw the light, too," Mike agreed.

"We need to see what's going on inside," Dana chimed in. "Let me out here, and I'll take a look."

"Not without me." Mitch didn't want her to go anywhere near the place. He stopped at the stop sign at the end of the street, planning to circle around the block.

Mike chose that moment to push his door open. "Pick me up in five minutes."

"Wait…" he started but it was too late. Mike slammed the door and ran lightly toward the building.

Mitch blew out a breath and turned left. Dana reached out to grasp his arm. "Do you see that guy?"

"Who?" He squinted through the rain and saw who she meant. A man wearing a black raincoat and a hat strode across the street to a parking lot where a large black Cadillac Escalade was sitting. "Does he look familiar to you?"

Dana didn't respond, her gaze focused out her passenger-side window. He needed to watch the road, but took his time making the turn.

"I don't believe it," Dana whispered.

His gut clenched. "What?"

"That's Oliver Shelton," Dana said.

"Are you sure?" He wanted to believe her, but it was dark and raining, and she'd admitted she hadn't met the guy often.

"Yes, positive. Oliver looks even more like Alice than he did before. But I don't understand—the building is still owned by Chicago Land Corp., right? So why is he here?"

"Maybe he's more involved with the owners of Chicago Land than we thought." Mitch didn't like the implication.

"Slow down, there's Mike."

He hit the brakes and unlocked the doors. Mike ducked inside, his wet hair plastered against his head and his dark T-shirt soaked to the skin. "Dana was right, they're definitely making drugs. I could see chemistry-type equipment and white powder."

Mitch met his brother's gaze in the rearview mirror. "We need to let Miles know." He quickly dialed Miles's number.

Just as his brother answered, "Hello?" there was a loud noise that sounded suspiciously like a gunshot.

Someone was shooting at them from the warehouse!

SIXTEEN

A *gunshot*? Before Dana could react, three men swarmed out of the warehouse back door, instantly surrounding their SUV in the front and on both sides, handguns held ready.

From the corner of her eye, she saw Mitch swiftly tuck his phone into the front pocket of his jeans.

"Hands up! Get out of the car!" the tall guy standing directly in front of their SUV yelled.

Dana's stomach clenched with fear and she silently began to pray. *Dear Lord, help us! Keep us safe!*

"Okay, okay!" Mitch held his arms up palms forward in a gesture of surrender. "Don't shoot! We're coming out!"

"Are you nuts?" Mike asked in a harsh whisper.

"You have a better idea?" Mitch countered in a low voice. The rain pelting against the hood of the car helped keep their conversation private. "The only option we have is to stall for as long as possible." Raising his voice, he said again, "We're coming out!" Slowly, he pulled the door latch, then kicked it the rest of the way open with his foot.

Dana mimicked his motions on her side and stepped out into the deluge. The sky brightened with a shaft of lightning followed by a long rumble of thunder as the storm gathered intensity.

The rain pelted against her thin cotton blouse, instantly soaking her to the skin. Her jeans offered little protection, either, and despite the warm, muggy temperatures, she shivered.

"Oliver Shelton asked us to check out this warehouse on Riverbend and Morgan," Mitch said. "This is the right place, isn't it?"

Dana stood outside the SUV, far too close to the third man holding a gun. She couldn't see his features clearly because of the water running into her face, and she hoped he wasn't smart enough to figure out how Mitch was giving clues to his brother Miles on the other end of the open phone line.

Smart move on Mitch's part, yet she was afraid that Miles would be too late.

What was to stop these men from shooting them once they were inside the warehouse?

She couldn't think of a single thing.

Stall for as long as possible.

"I'm Dana Petrie and I was married to Kent Petrie," she said in a loud voice so that she could be heard over the storm. "Alice Shelton's son. They love me like a daughter, and they won't be happy if you hurt me."

She felt Mike come up to stand beside her. "She's right," he added in a rough tone. "She's an integral part of the Shelton family. We're not here to interfere with your job."

A couple of the gunmen exchanged looks as if silently debating if they should believe Dana's claim. "Get moving," the guy closest to her said, waving his gun at the front of the car.

Swallowing hard, she edged around the hood of the

SUV, trying to stay as far away as possible from the gunmen. As soon as she was close to Mitch, he reached out and drew her against him. Mike joined them, and she was sandwiched protectively between the two Callahans. Mitch's warm presence was reassuring, and infused her with a sense of strength.

They could do this.

They *had* to do this.

"Should I call Alice now?" she volunteered. "I'm sure my mother-in-law would be happy to vouch for me."

"You should let her call," Mitch added. "That way we can clear up any confusion."

"Shut up and get inside," the guy near Mitch said.

Surrounded as they were, there was little choice but to move toward the side door of the warehouse. Dana walked slowly, worried that once they got inside, their chance for escape would be over. Another lightning bolt shot across the sky, followed by a sharp crack of thunder, causing the guy nearest to Dana to reflexively hunch his shoulders as if he was afraid of the storm.

Was there some way to use that against him? She glanced at Mitch, wondering if he'd noticed the guy's reaction, but she couldn't tell by the grim expression on his face.

Then it was too late as they were pushed across the threshold and into the building. The place had a musty smell intermixed with a stringent chemical scent.

She wrinkled her nose, trying to hold back a sneeze. As Mike mentioned, there was clearly drug manufacturing going on in the open space. Plastic gloves and face masks had been discarded in a hurry, likely by the gunmen. The guys must be doing double duty, creating drugs while protecting the place. There was also a large container of a white powdery substance in the center of an old metal table, and her chest tightened with fear and worry at how much carfentanil was inside.

Even a milligram could be enough to kill someone who didn't have an opiate tolerance built up. The amount sitting there could kill an army of people.

Stall for as long as possible.

"Now what?" Mitch asked. "What do you plan to do? Kill us with your superstrength narcotic?"

"Exactly," the tallest of them said. He was the one who had stood directly in front of their SUV and the obvious leader.

They couldn't just stand there and let these men inject them with carfentanil. At least there weren't more men inside the warehouse that she could see. Still, three armed men against two men and a woman with only one gun wasn't encouraging. Especially since the only gun she was aware of was the ankle holster that Mike had given Mitch.

Not exactly easy access to use in self-defense.

Dana strove for a casual tone. "You're going to do that without calling Alice or Oliver Shelton first? Big mistake."

The leader seemed to hesitate for a fraction of a second, then grinned, without humor. His eyes narrowed with a hint of evil. "You think I'm worried about offending old man Ollie? He's afraid of us, not the other way around. We're in charge here."

"Yeah, right," she scoffed, calling his bluff. At least, she hoped he was bluffing. Because if he was right and the Sheltons were the ones who owed these guys and were in fact taking orders from them, then she and the Callahan brothers were in trouble.

Big trouble.

A few months ago, it wouldn't have mattered. She hadn't had much to live for, simply going through the motions without experiencing a sense of joy or wonder.

But now she had Mitch, who'd shown her that the future wasn't as bleak as she'd once thought. Not only had he opened her heart and her mind to a renewed faith in God, he'd given her a second chance at love.

If they survived long enough to explore the possibility.

She glanced at Mitch, wondering how much longer they could postpone the inevitable. Was Miles was still listening in and already on his way to their rescue?

Please, Lord, bring Miles soon.

Because she wanted that second chance. More than anything.

Come on, Miles, any time, Mitch thought. He wasn't sure how much longer they could stall.

He suspected Mike still had a gun, no doubt his brother owned several, and he still had Mike's thirty-eight in the ankle holster. But once the gunmen patted them down, it would be all over.

Then they would have no way to defend themselves against bullets or, worse, against the superstrength narcotic.

How much time had passed since he'd connected with Miles? Five minutes? Seven at the most?

If Miles didn't show up soon, he'd have to risk going for the ankle holster. Mitch didn't see any other way around it. If he caused enough of a commotion, maybe Mike could get Dana out of there.

He glanced at his brother then down to his foot, in an attempt to make him understand his intent. Mike narrowed his gaze, as if telling him it was a lousy plan, and Mitch couldn't necessarily disagree.

"Get three needles and syringes," the guy in charge said.

The other two men glanced at each other, then the one closest to the metal table tucked his gun in his waistband and went over to a small box of supplies.

Interesting. Making their deaths look like accidental overdoses wasn't the smartest move. They didn't have existing needle tracks that a typical user would.

As if the guy had read Mitch's mind, he abruptly said, "Wait, forget the needles. We'll make them snort it instead."

"No one is going to believe all three of us just decided to start using drugs," Dana said, a hint of terror underlying her tone. "I'm telling you, we work for the Sheltons. You don't have anything to fear from us."

The leader leered at her and took a step forward. "I think you'll go first," he said in a snide tone. "So that the other two can watch you die."

No! He couldn't bear it!

Mitch instinctively took a step toward Dana, only to have the second gunman abruptly lift his weapon and point it directly at his chest in the region of his heart.

"Don't move," the guy said. "We'll shoot if necessary. It'll be easy enough to bury your bodies where they'll never be found."

Mitch curled his fingers into fists, battling a wave of helplessness. The guy at the metal table pulled on the gloves then used a putty knife to scrape a small amount of white powder in the palm of his hand.

"This is for you, little lady," he said, carefully stepping toward Dana. "Don't worry, you won't feel a thing."

When he lifted his palm dangerously close to Dana's

face, Mitch knew he couldn't wait another second. With a silent prayer asking for God's strength and endurance, he dropped to one knee and scrabbled for the thirty-eight.

Simultaneously, there was a loud bang from the side door of the warehouse. In the back of his mind, Mitch assumed the building was hit by lightning and used the distraction to pull his weapon from the holster and leap back up to his feet.

He aimed at the leader, hoping that if he wounded that guy, the others would fall into place.

"Put your hands in the air!" a familiar voice shouted.

Miles? Yes! And his brother had brought a full SWAT team with him.

The leader fired at Miles, who was thankfully wearing bulletproof gear. He missed and Mitch shot him in return. The leader screamed and fell to the ground.

Mike had a weapon in his hand, too, and joined the melee. As Mitch turned toward Dana, he was shocked when he saw her take a deep breath and blow with all her might at the white powder in the hand of the guy closest to her, spraying him in the face with the highly concentrated drug. He coughed and sputtered, staggered back and forth on his feet for a long couple of seconds, then fell to the ground.

Mike took out the third guy and then it was over. Miles crossed over to clap Mitch on the shoulder. "Good timing, bro," he said.

"Yeah." His hands had started to shake with the aftermath of adrenaline, so he carefully put the thirty-eight down on the ground. "I guess you have to arrest me now, huh?"

"We'll deal with that later," Miles assured him.

"Mitch?" Dana's voice was faint and tentative. He

spun toward her, and she swayed and began to crumple to the floor.

He grabbed her and managed to break her fall. "What is it? What's wrong?"

Her wide green eyes stared at him for a moment, her pupils big and dilated. Then he knew.

Some of the drug she'd blown toward the guy who'd tried to kill her must have been absorbed into her system, too. Maybe some had gotten into her nose or mouth by mistake.

"Call 911!" he shouted, cradling Dana to his chest. "She needs Narcan to counteract the narcotic!"

"There's an ambulance outside," Miles said. "They come on every SWAT call."

"Hurry!" Mitch tightened his grip on Dana, willing her not to die. "Hang on, Dana, hang on! You're going to be all right."

She didn't respond. Her face was pale and still and he panicked because she had stopped breathing.

"Hurry!" he screamed again as he gently laid her on the floor and began doing mouth-to-mouth resuscitation. He gave her several breaths then felt for a pulse.

It was there, but the rhythm was weak, and he feared she'd slip away before he could tell her how much he loved her.

Two paramedics arrived, pushing Mitch to the side so they could get access to Dana's extremities. "She needs to be treated for a narcotic overdose," he said. "These guys are making some superpowerful narcotic here and she was exposed to it."

The paramedic closest to him deftly placed a catheter in her vein and began infusing IV fluids. Then he began pulling up medication from a small glass vial while the other paramedic took vital signs.

"Narcan in," the paramedic said.

There was a long moment as they waited for Dana to respond.

Nothing.

"Give her more fluids and another dose," Mike said.

Mitch glanced at his brother in surprise.

"That's what they did for you in the ER," Mike said. "It took three doses of Narcan to bring you around."

"I know how to treat a narcotic overdose," the paramedic said in a dry tone. He drew up more medication from a second glass vial.

After the second dose, Dana responded. Her muscles twitched and she blinked, then opened her beautiful green eyes. "Mitch?"

"I'm here. You're fine. Everything is going to be all right." He bent down and pressed a kiss against her forehead, then silently thanked God for saving her life.

"She needs to get checked out at the hospital," the paramedic next to him said.

"No," Dana protested weakly. She looked up at him, but he wasn't sure she was really seeing him clearly.

"Yes, you do." Mitch wasn't about to stand in the way of her need to get the best care possible. He forced a smile. "We're safe now and there's no need to worry. Miles is here and he'll take care of everything."

"Okay." Her eyelids fluttered closed.

He tucked a strand of her wet hair behind her ear and pressed a sweet kiss on the center of her forehead. "I love you, Dana," he whispered.

She didn't respond, but he hoped she'd heard him. He forced himself to move out of the way so the two paramedics could get her onto the stretcher.

Mitch followed her out of the warehouse and into the rain, which had lessened to a mild drizzle, the worst of the storm having passed by. He would ride along in the ambulance for now; Mike could drive the SUV and meet him at the hospital.

From there? He figured Miles would come to question him. Which was fine with him.

After the way he'd almost gotten Dana and Mike killed, he was done running.

It was time to turn himself in.

SEVENTEEN

Hearing the sound of muted voices, Dana forced her heavy eyelids open. The overhead lights were painfully bright, but someone must have noticed her wince, because they abruptly dimmed.

Much better. She blinked and focused on Mitch's concerned expression as he leaned over her. "How are you feeling?"

"Weak," she answered truthfully. "Thirsty, but otherwise fine." It took a moment for her to realize she was on the wrong side of the bed in the ER where she worked. How mortifying to have her coworkers taking care of her. Mitch held up a cup of water for her to drink. When she finished, she struggled to sit upright. "I need to get out of here."

"Soon, but not yet," Mitch protested, putting a hand on her arm. "Dr. Robertson hasn't given the final okay yet."

"What time is it?" She squinted at the clock.

"Seven thirty in the evening."

Hours had passed, and they hadn't eaten since early that morning at the truck stop. No wonder she felt a little sick to her stomach.

"Mitch?" A tall man with brown hair and green eyes

wearing SWAT gear poked his head into the room. She recognized him as Mitch's older brother Miles. "We need to talk."

"I know. Give me a few minutes."

Dana frowned. "What's happening? Are you going to be arrested?"

Mitch's expression turned rueful. "I'm not sure, but try not to worry. Mike is here to keep you safe."

She appreciated Mike, but wanted to stay with Mitch. "Why can't we stick together?"

"I'm not the lead investigator here," Miles said from the doorway. "At some point the detective assigned to the case will need to interview you separately." He stepped into the room. "We busted a portion of the drug manufacturing and linked the men who were there to Chicago Land Corp., but do you guys have any proof related to who actually murdered Janice and Simon?"

"We have reason to believe Oliver Shelton is the guy calling the shots," Mitch said.

Dana nodded. "I saw him leaving the warehouse and getting into his fancy car. Why else would he be there if he wasn't working with Chicago Land Corp.?"

"We think he buys the warehouses from them for a significant amount of money, at least on paper. He insures them for that same amount, starts construction, causes a fire, gets the money, then sells the damaged property for a loss."

Miles rubbed the back of his neck, his expression full of doubt. "Pretty elaborate scheme."

"Maybe, but there is a paper trail proving Shelton, Inc. buys the properties from Chicago Land," Dana said. "And we know at least one fire, the most recent one Mitch investigated, was caused by arson, not faulty wiring."

"And I have Jeff's notes where he wrote the initials *O.S.* for Oliver Shelton," Mitch added. "I think if you dig into Jeff's finances, you'll see that prior to his heart attack and untimely death, he had an influx of money that likely leads to Shelton."

"Nice theories, but who is the one doing the actual murders?" Miles asked. "Not Shelton himself."

"Tyler Pitrowski?" Dana glanced at Mitch. "Wasn't that the name of the cop's brother-in-law? The one who works security for Shelton, Inc.?"

"Yes. And we have the weapon you took from him," Mitch agreed. "If he left prints on the gun, we can prove he tried to kill us. He has a criminal record including a felony drug conviction."

"Your word against his." Miles's expression was gloomy. "But it's better than nothing."

"It's the whole picture," Mitch insisted. "And enough for reasonable doubt."

"Maybe." Miles didn't look enthusiastic. "But circumstantial evidence goes a long way. Do you know that the detective on your case found your work vehicle in your garage with Janice's blood in the trunk?"

Mitch groaned. "I was afraid of that. We looked, but couldn't find it. But you need to tell the forensic team to do a tight sweep of the vehicle, because the real killer could have left a hair or some other trace evidence behind."

"You think this Pitrowski guy is the one who set all this up? Murdered two people and framed you?" Miles asked.

"Why not?" Dana didn't understand the skepticism in Miles's tone. "He's related to a cop by marriage. Maybe he learned a few tricks along the way."

Mike stepped into the room. "The doc is on his way in to discharge Dana."

She was relieved to hear it, even though she didn't want to leave Mitch. There was a niggling worry in the back of her mind that they were still missing something, a connection.

But what?

"Mike, I need you to take Dana to Mom's," Mitch said. "Maybe stop and get her something to eat along the way."

"What about you?" she asked.

There was a long pause before Mitch met her gaze. "I'm letting Miles take me in."

"Why?" The minute she asked the question, she knew he was cooperating with Miles to protect her and his family.

"Take care of her," Mitch said, then abruptly turned away. "Let's go, Miles."

"Hold on," Miles said. "It's almost eight o'clock on a Saturday night. If you go in now, you'll sit in jail all weekend. I'll call my boss, promise to bring you in first thing Monday morning. He owes me a favor, and once I explain about the drug bust and the potential link to the murders, I'm sure he'll agree."

Dana's heart swelled in relief. "That would be wonderful."

"Here, take the rented SUV. I left it on the ground floor of the parking structure. I'll hitch a ride with Miles to pick up Hawk's SUV and the weapon Dana took from Pitrowski. We'll meet you at Mom and Nan's."

Dana gingerly sat up and swung her legs over the edge of the bed. Her soaked blouse and jeans were uncomfortable, but she noticed a fresh pair of scrubs sitting on the chair. She slid to her feet, held on to the bed rail for a moment to make sure she wouldn't fall, then took the scrubs and excused herself to go to the bathroom to change.

Wearing dry clothes felt wonderful. She joined Mitch, who reached out to take her hand in his. "Dr. Robertson said you were free to go. And he was nice enough to give me additional antibiotics since we left them behind."

"Good." She led the way through the ER, out the main entrance toward the parking structure. The sky was still overcast with dark clouds, but the rain had stopped, leaving the air cool and clear.

There weren't many people around, a little surprising for a Saturday night at the only level-one trauma center in the city. Several of the overhead parking structure lights were out, too, which was also odd.

As they neared the rented SUV, two people moved out of the shadows. "Put your hands up and be quiet or I'll shoot first and ask questions later."

Dana froze and recognized Alice Petrie and another guy who was about the same age as Mitch. He didn't look like Pitrowski, and her worst fears were confirmed when Mitch spoke.

"Paul Roscoe? But why? Was this your plan all along? To get the job as fire investigator so you could take over where Walker left off?"

Dana sucked in a breath, remembering the picture of Roscoe standing beside Simon. This was the connection they'd missed.

"Doesn't matter. You're both coming with us," the man named Roscoe said.

"Alice? Why?"

"You never appreciated how good you had it, did you, Dana?" Alice asked in a snide tone. "You weren't good enough for my son. He became a firefighter for you, and died because of it. You stole my son from me. You!"

The woman was crazy. She hadn't forced Kent to be a firefighter—that had been his own idea. And Shelton Inc. had been likely responsible for his death. And suddenly, Dana couldn't stand the idea of being in danger again. She knew there were cameras in the structure, but they were mostly on the main thoroughfares, and Roscoe and Alice were standing close enough in the shadow that she didn't think they'd be seen.

There were panic buttons, too. And if her memory served correctly, there was one about five yards behind her.

Without warning, she spun around and lunged for the panic button. She heard a shout from behind her as her palm hit the alarm, and instantly strobe lights flashed and sirens blared.

When she turned back around, she saw that Mitch was fighting with the man named Roscoe while Alice was attempting to escape. She ran toward Kent's mother, all the anger and frustration coming out as she screamed, "No!"

Alice was half in and half out of an expensive black car, similar to the one Oliver had used earlier, so Dana slammed against the door, pinning her where she was. Mitch had Roscoe on the ground, kicking the gun out of his reach.

Several hospital security guards and a Milwaukee County sheriff's deputy came running over to assist.

And then it was over. Roscoe and Alice were arrested and hauled away. Mitch pulled Dana into his arms, then glanced over at his two brothers who had come out to join them.

"Roscoe was the missing link," he said. "From the

beginning I suspected Simon because he was a fire-fighter, but when he turned up dead, I never considered there might be another firefighter involved. And Roscoe knew all about me and my relationship with Janice. I should have considered him a suspect earlier. Especially since he wanted to take over Walker's job."

"Why would you? This was good work, bro," Miles said with a grin. "Guess you've solved the case after all. Come on. Me and Mike will drive you home."

Dana wasn't sure she wanted to meet Mitch's family under these circumstances, but she didn't want to go back to the home Alice and Edward Shelton had purchased for her and Kent, either.

For now, she would have to accept the Callahans' hospitality. And maybe there would be some time for her and Mitch to talk about the future once they were alone.

Mitch loved his family, but hadn't anticipated the crowd waiting for them at his mom and Nan's house. Several cars lined the driveway, so he wasn't surprised to see that all of his siblings were there; even the newlyweds, Matt and Lacy, had returned from their honeymoon. Duchess, Matt's K-9 partner, wove between the family members, her wagging tail beating against them in greeting.

"Mitch!" His mother enveloped him in a warm embrace, then she turned and smiled at Dana. "Hi, I'm Margaret Callahan."

"Dana Petrie," she said in a faint tone.

"Everyone? Meet Dana Petrie." Mitch looked at the crowd of people in the kitchen. "Dana, this is my entire family. My mother and grandmother, Nan, live here. The rest are party crashers."

"Welcome to the madness," Mike said in a low tone.

Mitch ignored him. "I don't expect you to remember all their names, but the guy near the fridge is my oldest brother, Marc, and his wife, Kari, and their two kids, Max and baby Maggie. Then you have Miles's wife, Paige, and their daughter, Abby, and their new baby, Adam. He was born about a week after Maggie. You already met Noah, and he's standing next to his wife and my sister, Maddy. Matt is Maddy's twin and he's married to Lacy, and that's their son, Rory. Oh, and Duchess is Matt's K-9 partner." He glanced around the room. "I think that's it."

"It's nice to meet everyone," Dana said softly.

He glanced at her in concern. She looked pale and uncomfortable, as if this was all too much to handle after everything they'd been through.

"Hey, are you all right? Maybe you need something to eat," he said.

"No, please, I couldn't," Dana protested. "Um, please excuse me for a moment." Before he could figure out what was going on, she turned and ducked outside, the door shutting behind her with a loud click.

"Something we said?" Marc asked wryly.

Kari rolled her eyes and shifted Maggie to her other arm. "More likely she's simply overwhelmed from meeting us all at the same time. Not everyone is used to being around a large family."

"You managed to get used to it," Marc said, bending down to kiss her.

"I better check on her," Mitch said. "Excuse me." He headed outside, disturbed to find Dana walking down the driveway as if she intended to walk all the way back to her place.

"Dana, wait!" He jogged to catch up to her, appalled

to see streaks of tears down her cheeks. "What is it? What's wrong?"

She swiped at her face. "So many babies," she whispered. "I don't think I can stay here."

Babies? He didn't understand. "They'll all head home soon. Only you and I are staying overnight."

"No, you don't get it. Your family is full of babies!" She drew a deep breath and turned to face him. "I suffered a miscarriage three years ago, on the day of Kent's funeral."

Now it all made sense. No wonder she'd locked her feelings away. She hadn't just lost a husband, she'd lost a family. "Oh, Dana, I'm so sorry." He pulled her into his arms, cradling her close. "I can't imagine how terrible that must have been, losing your child right after your husband's death. I'm sure the Petries were supportive."

Dana shook her head from side to side, her voice muffled against his chest. "I didn't tell them. I didn't tell anyone, ever. Until now."

"Sweetheart." He was humbled that she'd told him, but wasn't sure what to say to make her feel better.

"Those babies reminded me of what I've lost. I know it's not their fault, but it felt like a kick in the face seeing them so happy and healthy..." Her voice trailed off.

"I'm here for you, no matter what. Don't you understand? I love you. Please don't leave, not like this."

"Love?" She raised her head and looked up at him. "It's only been a few days."

"I know, and I'll give you all the time you need, but I love you, Dana. You're beautiful, smart and brave. You saved our lives back there going for the panic button. I'll give you space, but won't you consider giving a relationship with me a chance?"

"Oh, Mitch." The sorrow on her face sent a dagger

to his heart. "You deserve someone better than me. Someone who doesn't freak out at seeing happy babies."

"If I had known, I would have had my family leave before we arrived," he said. "You're what's important to me, Dana. I know my family can be overwhelming, but there's no rush. You'll have plenty of time to get used to them. Don't walk away from me, from us." He paused, then added, "From our future."

She didn't say anything for a long moment, then she lifted up on her tippy-toes and kissed him. He reveled in her kiss, cuddling her close while showing her without words how he truly felt about her. How much he hoped and prayed she'd give their love a chance to nurture and grow.

"Wow," she whispered, breaking off from their kiss and gasping for breath. "You sure make it difficult to think clearly."

"Thinking is overrated," he chided playfully.

She tipped her head to the side, regarding him thoughtfully. "Mitch, I need to be honest with you. It's not just the fact that I lost a baby. It's that I don't know why it happened. Stress? Could be, but I never bothered to get additional testing to see what the cause might have been." She hesitated, then added, "Maybe we should wait until I know more before we commit to anything further."

"No." He tightened his grip around her. "Dana, if you don't love me, that's one issue. But I love you and I want you no matter what medical problems you do or don't have."

"Are you sure?"

"Absolutely positive," he said without hesitation.

She smiled. "I'm glad. Because I love you, too, Mitch. Thanks for bringing me back to life and back to my faith."

"I'm the one who should be thanking you." He kissed her again, relieved to know that she was willing to take a chance.

With him.

EPILOGUE

Six weeks later...

Dana was running late, partially because they'd gotten a critically ill patient in just as her four-hour shift was about to end, then also because she'd taken the time to shower and change out of her scrubs in the woman's locker room.

She didn't like missing church services, but unfortunately weekend shifts were part of the job. And she was grateful that she was scheduled for only a half shift, which meant she was still able to join the family brunch.

The drive to the Callahans didn't take too long, although the driveway was already lined with cars. No doubt she was the last to arrive. She hurried into the kitchen, where a few of the wives were gathered. She greeted Mitch's mom with an apologetic smile. "Sorry I'm late. Is there something I can do to help?"

"Hi, dear." Mitch's mother gave her a quick hug. Dana had learned the woman hugged everyone, and secretly loved being included. Margaret Callahan's warmth reminded her of her grandmother. "I think we're about ready."

"Dana, can you take Maggie for a minute?" Kari

thrust the squirmy pink bundle into Dana's arms. "I'll be right back."

"Um, sure." Nonplussed, she looked down into the wide blue eyes of the little girl. Maggie smiled and waved her arms as if she wanted to say something, but couldn't.

It was the first time she'd held any of the Callahan babies, and at this moment, she realized how foolish she'd been to avoid it for so long.

Her baby was gone, but that didn't mean life didn't go on. The Callahan clan was proof of that. And how could anyone resist the smallest members of the family? One of Maggie's hands lightly batted her cheek, making her smile.

"You have to save that move for when a little boy gets too close, right?"

Maggie smiled as if understanding her words.

"Thanks," Kari said, returning to pluck the baby out of Dana's arms. "Mitch said to send you into the living room."

"If you're sure you don't need any help." Dana looked at Mitch's mom for confirmation.

"Go ahead, tell everyone brunch is ready."

"Dana!" Mitch looked delighted to see her. He leaped from his seat and came over to give her a hug and a kiss. "Glad you made it."

"Of course." She blushed, still not accustomed to Mitch's displays of affection in front of his family. Not that anyone seemed to notice. "Your mom said brunch is ready."

"Best not to keep Mom waiting," Miles said, easing past her.

"Mitch, the DA's office is bringing the case against Alice Petrie, Oliver Shelton, Paul Roscoe and Tyler

Pitrowski—his prints were officially identified on the gun used to try to kill you—to the grand jury next week," Maddy said, squeezing in beside Noah. "We think it's just a matter of time before they start turning against each other in hopes of getting a lighter sentence."

Dana was glad to know Mitch's name had been cleared once and for all. And given Alice's impending indictment, and Edward's involvement in the deals as well, she had decided to sell the house and to donate most of the proceeds to a new drug addiction rehab facility.

It was the least she could do make amends for the horrible drug manufacturing her former husband's family had been secretly supporting.

The meal was noisy, fun and wonderful. Afterward, she jumped up to help clear away the dirty dishes, since she hadn't been there to help cook, but Margaret Callahan and Nan shooed her away.

"Dana, will you come outside and take a walk with me?" Mitch asked.

"Sure." She should have insisted on staying to help, but she took Mitch's hand and followed him out into the sunny summer day. He headed out into the backyard, where there was a swing beneath the trees, wide enough for two.

She sat and scooted over so he could sit next to her, but he didn't. Instead, he dropped to one knee and took her hands in his.

"Dana, over these past six weeks, I've learned to love you more than ever. The way you stood beside me while I cleared my name makes me realize I can't live without you. Will you please marry me?"

Her eyes filled with tears that she tried to blink away.

"Oh, Mitch, I love you, too. And I don't want to think about what my life would be like without you, so yes. Yes, I'd be honored to marry you."

He pulled out a ring, but her vision was too blurry to see it clearly and she didn't really care. Whatever he'd gotten for her, she'd love and wear the rest of her life.

"I love you, Dana." He stood and pulled her to her feet. "I don't need a family if that's too much for you. All I need is you."

He kissed her, and after several minutes she pulled away to breathe and to look up into his handsome face. "Mitch, I love you, too, and I want to have a family with you. If it's part of God's plan."

"There's no rush, Dana," he said, concern darkening his blue eyes. "I want you to be sure. I'll be happy enough with you."

That was the sweetest thing he could have said, but she knew her own heart and understood that his family was important to him. And to her. "I am sure. Very sure." She reached up to kiss him again, knowing he was the one she was destined to spend the rest of her life with.

Mitch and the rest of the Callahan family.

* * * * *

WE HOPE YOU ENJOYED THIS BOOK!

Love Inspired® SUSPENSE

Uncover the truth in these thrilling stories of faith in the face of crime from Love Inspired Suspense.

Discover six new books available every month at Barnes & Noble!

LISHALO2019BN

A movement outside caught Hawk's attention. He froze, his gaze tracking the shifting of leaves and the sudden uprising of a bird from the bushes.

Too late! They'd found the cabin.

He hurried into the bedroom as Jillian was trying to coax the teddy bear from Lizzy's grip. "We need to go. Get your coats, leave the duffel behind. We're heading out the back."

"The back?" The confusion in Jillian's green gaze morphed into fear. She instantly yanked the bear away, shoved Lizzy's coat on, then hers, before lifting Lizzy into her arms. She returned the teddy bear, hoping the stuffed animal would help keep Lizzy calm. Her voice dropped to a whisper. "They're here?"

He nodded, gently pulling her toward him. Ushering her into his bedroom and to the back doorway he had built in there just for this type of thing, he considered their options. First, they needed to get out of the cabin and deeper into the woods without leaving a blatant footprint trail behind. Using the SUV was out of the question; the hostiles were too close. He'd have to make do with the snowmobile he had hidden in the woods toward the back of his property.

Outside, the December air was crisp and cool despite the sunshine. Keeping Jillian in front of him, he covered their backs as he guided them into the woods. He could tell Jillian was trying to move silently, but to his ears it sounded as if they were a stampede of elephants announcing their location to anyone within a fifty-mile radius.

Thankfully, Lizzy didn't say anything but kept her head tucked against her mother's shoulder, still gripping the tattered teddy bear. He wished the little girl trusted him enough to allow him to carry her—they'd be able to move more quickly. But he didn't want to risk her tears.

Knowing the woods helped. The cluster of bushes he'd been aiming for was straight ahead. He picked up his pace. Jillian did her best to keep up, but her foot got caught on a branch. He managed to catch her before she hit the ground.

He gently set her on her feet and gestured toward the cluster of bushes. She nodded her understanding and headed in that direction. Hawk continued sweeping his gaze over the area, looking for signs the hostiles were near, surprised that they hadn't covered the backside of the cabin but had chosen to come in from the front and the west.

Although he knew there very well could be more.

When they reached the cluster of bushes, he carved out a small space with his hands and drew Jillian down. "Stay here. I'll be back soon."

She clutched at his arm. "Don't leave us," she begged.

It wasn't by choice but out of necessity. He leaned down so his mouth was near her ear. "I have a snowmobile nearby. I promise I'll be quick."

Tears welled in her eyes, but she gave a jerky nod, showing she understood. He drew out his gun and handed it to her. This time she didn't protest but clutched it with both hands while keeping one arm around Lizzy, holding her close.

He hesitated. There was so much he wanted to say, but there wasn't time. He needed to move, to draw the hostiles away from Jillian and Lizzy.

He'd willingly sacrifice himself to keep them alive and safe.

Don't miss
Soldier's Christmas Secrets *by Laura Scott,*
available November 2019 at Barnes & Noble!

LoveInspired.com

Discover wholesome and uplifting stories of faith, forgiveness and hope.

Join our social communities to connect with other readers who share your love!

Sign up for the Love Inspired newsletter at **LoveInspired.com** to be the first to find out about upcoming titles, special promotions and exclusive content.

CONNECT WITH US AT:

Facebook.com/groups/HarlequinConnection

 Facebook.com/LoveInspiredBooks

 Twitter.com/LoveInspiredBks